BLINDSPOT

MICHAEL MCBRIDE

Dark Regions Press
–2011–

FIRST TRADE PAPERBACK EDITION

Text © 2011 by Michael McBride

Cover art © 2011 by Wayne Miller

Editor and Publisher, Joe Morey

ISBN: 978-1-937128-21-0

Cover and Interior Design By
Stephen James Price
www.GenerationNextPublications.com

Dark Regions Press
PO Box 1264
Colusa, CA 95932
www.darkregions.com

ACKNOWLEDGMENT

Special Thanks to: Joe and Chris Morey; Wayne Miller; Stephen James Price; Gene O'Neill; Gord Rollo; Jeff Strand; my *amazing* family; and to all of my loyal readers, without whom, as always, this book would not exist.

DEDICATION

For Trenton, who marches to his own beat

THE BLIND SPOT TEST

A blind spot, or *scotoma*, is an obscuration of the visual field. The blind spot in the human eye, known in medical literature as the physiological blindspot or *punctum caecum*, is the small circular area in the retina where the optic nerve enters the eye. This optic disc is devoid of rods and cones and is insensitive to light. The lack of photoreceptor cells forces the brain to reconcile this gap in visual perception by essentially "making up" what the eye *should* be seeing based on information gathered from the other eye. Thus, we are entirely unaware of the presence of the blindspot…as long as visual stimulation is seamless.

Above, you'll notice a triangle on the left and a smiley face on the right. Cover your left eye and focus on the triangle using your right eye. With your left eye closed, slowly move closer to this page. At a certain point, the smiley face on the right will disappear. That's your blindspot. (Try the same thing with your right eye closed while focusing on the smiley face.)

Why does it vanish?

Because as far as your brain is concerned, if your eye can't see it, then it doesn't exist.

PROLOGUE

On September 10th, 1996, the United Nations General Assembly adopted the Comprehensive Nuclear Test-Ban Treaty, which expressly prohibits all nuclear detonations in all environments, whether for military or civilian research purposes. While more than eighty countries—including five of the eight superpowers with nuclear capabilities—signed the treaty, the number that actually ratified it fell short of the minimum required for it to enter into force. However, the treaty did pave the way for the creation of the International Monitoring System, a worldwide network of 337 observation stations designed to detect nuclear detonations, under the oversight of the International Data Centre in Vienna, Austria. These stations are equipped to record and interpret sound waves traveling through the ground, the seas, and the sky, while simultaneously sampling the air for trace amounts of radioactive gasses and particles. Analysis of the seismic data allows for the rapid triangulation of the location of the detonation, as well as for the determination of its depth and magnitude.

Three days ago, on May 8th, seismic monitoring stations at Mudanjiang in northeast China and Teajon in the Republic of Korea—South Korea—detected a magnitude-4 event at precisely 2:31 a.m. Korea Standard Time (KST). Within minutes, the IDC triangulated the location of the detonation to a point in the southeastern corner of the Democratic People's Republic of Korea—North Korea—within the Korean Demilitarized Zone, which forms a buffer along the border between the two nations. The event occurred far from the known launch sites in Musudan-ri and Tongchang-dong and the uranium enrichment facility in Yongbyon, corroborating the U.N. Security Council's fears that Supreme Leader Kim Jong-un had indeed commissioned the construction of a series of secret nuclear manufacturing and testing sites, despite vehement protestations from North Korean officials, who insisted they produced only low-yield uranium for peaceful purposes. Satellite surveillance confirmed the appearance of what was described as a "golden flash" at that precise location and sporadic eyewitness accounts detailed a diffuse yellow-orange glow against the horizon, leading to speculation that after three unsuccessful attempts, the Taepodong-2 long-range missile was not only viable, but had been modified to deliver a nuclear payload.

At 8:00 a.m. KST, Kim Jong-un, dressed in full military uniform and in his capacity as Supreme Commander of the Korean People's Army, held a televised press conference during which he denied any foreknowledge of or responsibility for the detonation and shifted the blame onto his nemesis, Lee Myung-bak, President of the Republic of Korea, whom he accused of launching a strike against his country in delayed retaliation for the sinking of the South Korean warship Cheonan *and the bombardment of Yeonpyeong Island. Lee Myung-bak's only public response was a highly visible scrambling of troops—which included the dispatch of a dozen Pohang- and Donghae-class naval vessels and a submarine flotilla into the Yellow Sea to the east and the Sea of Japan to the west—and a call for support from the United Nations, whose foreign emissaries were already in the process of evacuating embassies throughout Pyongyang. With tensions flaring, North Korean refugees flooded the borders and erected impromptu camps along both the southern border, where they sought asylum within the Republic, and the Chinese border to the north, where a nervous Hu Jintao, whose country would be potentially decimated by the nuclear fallout should outright war erupt, stood prepared to launch a preemptive offensive that pundits believed could signal the beginning of a global offensive by one of the most powerful empires in the history of mankind.*

On May 9th, in a last minute attempt to avert catastrophe, the U.N. Security Council dispatched an elite unit of peacekeepers into the Taebaek Mountains from Kansŏng, ROK, under a cloak of secrecy. Its mission was to cross the border, penetrate the shroud of dust that prevented satellite visualization of the detonation site, and determine exactly what happened before the first shots heralding the commencement of World War III were fired.

Thirty-six hours later, Security Council President Anders Odegaard of Norway fielded a call on a secure satellite uplink. He, in turn, placed a call to a man at the Pentagon, who assured him that the U.S. Department of Defense would make all of the necessary arrangements.

Within two hours, a biomedical engineer from the United States Army Medical Research and Materiel Command, USAMRMC, boarded a fully fueled transport carrier at Ft. Detrick in Maryland.

The man's name is Dr. Parker Ramsey.

This is his story.

I

United States Army Bioengineering
Research & Development Laboratory

Ft. Detrick, Maryland

May 11

2:03 a.m. EST

(3:03 p.m. KST)

Dr. Parker Ramsey walked down the dark hallway toward his lab, careful not to slosh the scalding coffee from his mug onto the back of his hand. Light crept across the tiles from the cracks beneath the doors of a few scattered offices. Otherwise, the building was deserted. The place wouldn't come to life for nearly another five hours, but he'd been too excited to sleep. Rather than flop restlessly in his bed waiting for the first hint of the rising sun to slip through the blinds, he'd given up the battle and headed into his office to make sure that absolutely everything was in place and ready to go for the hundredth time. He'd been waiting for this day for so long that he should have known he didn't have a prayer of sleeping. His whole career—his entire life, for that matter—had been building up to this one day. All of those years in school, all of the hours spent in his tiny lab, and all of the sacrifices he had made in his personal life were finally about to pay off. Assuming everything functioned like it was supposed to, of course. But there was no cause for uncertainty. His research and preparations were meticulous. There was no doubt in his mind...

This was going to work.

He flicked on the light in his office, rounded his gray utilitarian desk, and set down his mug beside the keyboard. The pink copy of the bill of lading was taped to the computer monitor, just as he had expected. The delivery had been received less than thirty minutes ago. He smiled at the itemized list and imagined the expressions on the faces of some poor staff sergeant and his men as they toted a dozen coolers containing the heads of freshly butchered sheep into the refrigeration unit and unloaded them into the waiting specimen cases. The thought made him chuckle out loud.

"What's so funny?" a voice asked from the doorway.

Ramsey blushed and glanced up to see the very same staff sergeant—SSgt. Andrew Corvo—who was the source of his amusement. Judging by the expression on Corvo's face, he didn't find the situation nearly as comical. He held his rubber-gloved hands up and away from his body like a surgeon. They were positively dripping with blood. Ramsey tried not to stare at the vile crimson smudge on the man's cheek.

"What can I do for you, Sergeant?"

"Your decapitated heads are all in the fridge. I should probably thank you for helping me start my day in such a wonderful fashion, but I suppose it would be unfair to complain to you. At least the MG hasn't been sitting in his office for the last fifteen minutes waiting for me to drag my weary ass in here."

Ramsey felt the blood drain from his head. The room tilted on an invisible fulcrum.

Corvo smirked and disappeared back into the corridor.

For the first time, Ramsey noticed the flashing red message light on his phone, which rang as he was staring at it. He physically couldn't force himself to raise his arm to answer it. He just needed a moment to compose himself. What the hell was the major general doing here at all, let alone at two in the morning? As Commander of the United States Army Medical Research and Materiel Command,

Major General Thomas Aldridge, MD's role was largely administrative rather than supervisory. He rarely spent more than a few days a month at Ft. Detrick, and they were all given plenty of time to prepare themselves for his arrival. Ramsey couldn't think of a single instance when the MG had shown up unannounced, and he'd certainly never seen him in his office this early. Christ, Ramsey didn't even think the MG knew who he was.

The phone stopped ringing as the call was forwarded to his voicemail.

This was bad. This was very bad. He could only think of two reasons why Aldridge would want to talk to him on this of all days. Either the MG intended to make his presence felt at the formal testing of Ramsey's project to justify the enormous expenditure or he was here to terminate the project on the eve of Ramsey's greatest triumph. What if the testing didn't go as planned? What if he never had the opportunity to try? What then?

Ramsey's stomach turned sour.

The phone started to ring again. By now Aldridge undoubtedly knew he was here.

He swallowed hard and attempted to steady his voice when he answered.

"Dr. Parker Ramsey." His heart trilled like a hummingbird's. "Yes, sir. I'll be right up."

He hung up the phone and rose on unsteady legs. The walls seemed to close in upon him as he headed down the hallway toward the elevator and his date with destiny.

~*~

Ramsey scrutinized his warped reflection in the stainless steel elevator doors. His chestnut hair was still damp from the shower and his blue eyes were rimmed with red. He buttoned his crisp white lab coat to hide his wrinkled button-down, adjusted his tie, and smoothed the uneven creases in his slacks. Not how he would have chosen to meet with the major general by any stretch of the imagination, but what were the chances that his ultimate fate would be determined by his appearance this early in the morning anyway?

The bell signaling his arrival on the top floor chimed.

Ramsey drew a deep breath and stared between the opening doors into the deserted corridor. Through sheer force of will, he exited the elevator and headed directly for the Commander's Office, from which an industrial-white fluorescent glow emanated.

His heart rate accelerated with every step. There were snakes squirming in his guts and he only prayed his nerves wouldn't betray him. The last thing he wanted was to absolve himself of his breakfast in front of Aldridge.

The reception area was vacant, the desk unattended, the flags, paintings and photographs, and unit and command insignia on the walls shadowed. The plush chairs were so immaculate that it didn't look as though anyone had ever sat in them. He heard hushed voices from behind the partially closed door at the rear of the room, through which the sole light beckoned.

Ramsey cleared his throat and the door swung open. He immediately recognized Colonel David Cobb, Commander of the subordinate Materiel Management subunit, his more-or-less direct supervisor. Dave nodded a formal greeting, stepped to the side to allow him to enter, and then slipped out of the office. Ramsey caught a glimpse of the nervous expression on Dave's face through the gap in the closing door. When he turned again to face the room, Aldridge was staring holes through him from where he sat behind his antique desk. The computer monitor and keyboard had been shoved aside, along with the framed photographs of the MG shaking hands with two generations of presidents, to clear space for a stack of folders stamped with the words "Classified: Eyes Only" in red letters.

Aldridge followed Ramsey's gaze to the folders and gestured for him to sit in the chair opposite him with a sweep of his hand.

Ramsey eased into the seat and raised his eyes to meet the MG's. Aldridge was in his mid-sixties, but still looked like the man about whom stories of bare-knuckled fights in the back alleys of Saigon circulated. Maybe his face betrayed his age, and his hair was lighter and thinner than in the pictures before him, but he still struck a formidable presence. Add to that the fact that he was a brilliant surgeon who had pioneered the use of a sterile granulated composite initially manufactured from purified pork skins and sodium chloride to stop arterial bleeding in the field, and he was just about the most intimidating man that Ramsey had ever met.

Aldridge steepled his fingers under his chin and rocked slowly back and forth in his black leather chair, marring the seemingly interminable silence with a metronomic *creak...creak...creak.*

"I understand you served a tour of duty in Afghanistan, Dr. Ramsey," he finally said.

Ramsey could see the mechanisms grinding behind the MG's eyes. He was building up to something big, but he needed to satisfy whatever doubts plagued him first.

"249th Engineer Battalion, sir. Infrastructure. That was nearly a decade ago. Before I pursued my doctorate."

"In bioengineering. Stanford, correct? Not a cheap school, is it? God save the G.I. Bill. But you're no longer active duty, correct?"

"Civilian service, sir."

"Bigger check, same benefits. Smart man."

"Sir, that's not necessarily why I—"

"You're still in good shape. Excellent. And no medical conditions you've been keeping from us?"

"Sir?"

"Can you still handle a firearm?"

The question caught Ramsey off-guard. He opened his mouth to reply, but no sound came out. For the life of him, he couldn't figure out where this conversation was headed, but judging by the intensity of Aldridge's stare, the answer to the question was of the utmost importance.

"It's been years since I was last on a firing range."

"We aren't debating quantum theory here, Dr. Ramsey. Either you can or you can't."

Ramsey tried to read Aldridge's intent in his expression, but the man's face remained studiously neutral.

"Yes, sir. I believe I can still handle a firearm."

Aldridge plowed ahead as if he hadn't heard. To what end, however, Ramsey didn't have the slightest clue.

"Your project—Code Name Hindsight—is fully functional, is it not?"

"We'll find out soon enough."

"According to Colonel Cobb, Project Hindsight is complete and ready for field testing."

"We still have a ways to go. We're only now initiating the second phase of testing—"

"Does the goddamn thing work or not, Dr. Ramsey?" Aldridge shouted, slamming his open palm onto the desk.

Ramsey flinched and sank as far as he could into the chair to create distance between them. Aldridge's dramatic change in demeanor had come out of nowhere. His face was hot and red, his eyes as cold and blue as ice. His nostrils flared and his shoulders heaved. It appeared as though whatever semblance of control he maintained over the situation was tenuous at best.

This was the crux of the matter, wasn't it? But Ramsey couldn't seem to grasp the relationship between his research and the obvious pressure being exerted upon the major general, which had to be considerably more than merely financial in origin. All he knew with any kind of certainty was that however he answered the question, the course of his life was about to be altered in ways he could neither foresee nor forestall.

Ramsey licked his lips and stared at Aldridge for a long moment before he finally spoke.

"Sir, early experimentation on mice and rats demonstrated promising results, as I'm sure you know, but their anatomy and physiology differ so profoundly from our own that it would be irresponsible to proclaim success. Sheep are a different story, though. In this particular instance, they more closely resemble human—"

"You were scheduled to test the sheep this morning, correct?"

"'Were'?"

"Do you believe your experiment would have worked?"

"Yes, sir, but—"

"And when you proved your success and validated your results, you would have sought approval to initiate human testing."

"Sir—"

"Then you'll undoubtedly be pleased to learn that you've been given the green light to accelerate your timetable."

"I'm not sure I completely understand what you're—"

"You'll be briefed on the plane, Dr. Ramsey."

"Plane? With all due respect, sir, what in God's name are you talking about?"

‖

The black Bell UH-1 Iroquois came in so low over the tops of the evergreens that Ramsey instinctively lifted his feet. He glanced out the window to his right, half expecting to see an explosion of needles and bark from the rotors. Instead, he saw the pointed crowns of Olga Bay larches, Manchurian firs, and Jerzo spruces reaching from the steep slope, framed against the night sky. Massive granite slabs perched in their midst like dominos poised to topple down upon the valley into which they descended, where an ancient Buddhist temple crouched in a field filled with scrub oak and tall grasses that rippled with golden waves in the moonlight.

He didn't know exactly what he had expected, but this was just about the furthest thing from it.

"This is your drop, Dr. Ramsey," the pilot said through the cans on his ears. They were the first words he had spoken since they took off from Kansŏng, despite Ramsey's best attempts to coax him into telling where in the hell they were actually going.

"This can't be right," Ramsey said. "They don't really expect us to get out here, do they?"

"'Us'?"

The pilot's laughter was so loud that Ramsey had to remove the cans.

~*~

Within minutes of his conversation with Major General Aldridge, Ramsey was escorted to a transport carrier that had begun to taxi down the runway before the door even closed behind him. A lieutenant named Gibbons had presented him with leather-on-nylon, Gore-Tex-lined boots and camouflage fatigues, a rucksack containing a hydro bladder, dry rations and supplies, a camo CBRN over-suit, a charcoal-activated respirator, a gas mask, and a sealed folder that looked just like the ones on the MG's desk. He had denied any knowledge of the contents and excused himself from the cabin when Ramsey opened it. All he had volunteered was that his orders were to supervise the safe transport of sensitive cargo to a secure landing site in Kansŏng, a coastal town on the Sea of Japan, roughly forty-five kilometers south of the Korean Demilitarized Zone, where a Huey would be waiting to ferry the cargo to its ultimate destination. While Ramsey didn't necessarily appreciate continually being referred to as "the cargo," at least Gibbons had been kind enough to share his portable DVD player and his limited library of bad comedies, which helped distract Ramsey from dwelling on the contents of the folder.

He had read every page of text—all three of them—at least a dozen times and still knew little more than he had upon boarding. The phrasing was cryptic, the meanings implied, and the details non-existent. There was more written between the lines than in the lines themselves. If he understood correctly, both he and the equipment from his lab, which was presumably somewhere on the plane, were to be routed by helicopter from Kansŏng to an undisclosed rendezvous point of which the chopper pilot would only be informed after takeoff. There was no mention of their ultimate destination—which, Ramsey estimated, based on the Huey's range, could be anywhere within a three hundred mile radius—or what or whom would be waiting when he arrived, only that further orders would be provided at that time.

All Ramsey could do was speculate.

He knew he would be expected to utilize his project to some end. Based on his limited conversation with Aldridge and his briefing, he believed it would be on a human subject, but why were they flying him to the other side of the globe to conduct the experiment? To circumvent international human testing prohibitions? And why South Korea? He wasn't the kind of guy who immersed himself in politics and current affairs, but he'd heard enough to understand that he'd pretty much rather be just about anywhere else on the planet. A part of him had to admit that he was thrilled at the prospect of using his project on a human subject, though. He imagined himself setting up in a makeshift lab on one of the various Air Force bases or in the basement of an embassy, waiting for the body to be wheeled in so they could learn what the subject had seen that was of such dire importance.

But he couldn't shake Aldridge's question—*Can you still handle a firearm?*—or the simple and undeniable fact that he'd never been so scared in his entire life.

~*~

Now, here he was, fourteen hours later and halfway around the world, dressed in combat fatigues and preparing to alight in an isolated valley in the middle of the Taebaek Mountain Range where there wasn't another soul in sight.

What the Sam Hill was going on here?

The helicopter bounced when it touched down. Before it even settled, the door beside Ramsey slid back and he was hauled out into the furious wind and the grass whipping around his legs. He barely caught a glimpse of a man with a black grease-painted face before the man's grip tightened on his arm and they were ducking and running toward the small pagoda. The chopper rose with a roar into the sky behind them. By the time Ramsey looked back, it was cresting the mountains to the south, the thupping sound of its blades echoing into oblivion.

And then it was gone.

Without him.

They raced up the steps and into the small temple, which consisted of little more than a single room with cracked slate floors and petrified wooden support pillars. There were no windows or alternate egresses. The sparse moonlight from the doorway illuminated cracked images of the Buddha and praying disciples painted directly on the walls with an almost ethereal glow. A sculpture of the Buddha framed by a corona of flames rested in an arched hollow in the wall above a plain granite altar upon which several pots filled with sand, like old industrial ash trays, rested. The room was rife with the stale aroma of the snubbed incense sticks that protruded from the pots.

Ramsey gasped when two men materialized from the shadowed corners at the head of the room. All he could clearly see were the whites of their eyes. Another man entered the temple behind him without making a sound, his presence felt rather than seen. When Ramsey turned around, he saw that the man carried the two Pelican Storm Cases from his lab that had been custom-fitted with foam inserts to accommodate his equipment.

Four men, all taking his measure, staring at him as though waiting for him to do whatever it was he was supposed to do. And Ramsey didn't have the foggiest idea of what that was. He decided to take the direct approach.

"So where should I set up?"

The man who had led him from the chopper looked to each of the other men in turn, and then finally back at Ramsey. With their helmets pulled down low over their painted faces and nearly indistinguishable physiques, they could have passed for quadruplets. The man offered a crooked smile that could have passed for amusement, his ivory teeth a stark contrast to his features. And still he said nothing, so Ramsey kept going.

"I trust the subject is somewhere around here. Why don't we get this show on the road so we can bring the chopper back and I can return to—?"

The smiling man thrust the backpack Ramsey had been issued on the plane into his chest.

"I hope you brought a comfortable pair of shoes, princess," he said in a deep voice that contained just the hint of a Southern accent.

The other three grinned and suddenly Ramsey knew how Alice would have felt had she fallen through the looking glass and found herself surrounded by a rabid pack of Cheshire cats.

III

Ramsey had no idea how long they'd been walking, but the sky, when he actually stole a glimpse of it through the dense canopy, had begun to lighten to the east, if only by degree, which allowed him to gather his bearings. They were traveling northwest, single-file, following the topography of the steep valleys without ever straying from the cover of the trees. A stream paralleled them to their left, mocking them with its incessant babbling, but only occasionally revealing itself through the shrubs, branches, and trunks, a mere glimmer of moonlight on its silver surface.

They passed sheer cliffs where waterfalls fired from mist-shrouded bushes high above; dry creek beds where smooth stones had been stacked into gravity-defying cairns; twenty-foot-tall statues of the Buddha that appeared as if by magic from the forest; and the ruins of ancient dwellings long since claimed by the trees, which grew so closely together that their branches battled for the sunlight even as their roots waged war for the soil. The Taebaek Mountains were a world unto themselves, their beauty enhanced by their isolation. The detritus underfoot was pristine, as though no living being had ever dared to violate its eternal accumulation. Ramsey studied the sharp peaks high above him and the encroachment of the wilderness in an effort to divine their destination. All he could determine with any sort of accuracy was that if they continued on their current course, they would eventually breach the demilitarized zone and cross the border into North Korea, if they hadn't already. He wished the men would tell him where they were going, but none of them had spoken to him since offering clipped introductions as they set out from the temple, and his feeble attempts to draw them into conversation had been met with looks that could have dropped a charging rhino in its tracks.

He had been with them long enough now to be able to differentiate them. Rockwell was the man who had dragged him from the chopper, and appeared to be in command. He assumed the point and moved through the foliage a dozen paces ahead of them like an apparition. He was perhaps a couple of inches taller than the rest of them, had a square jaw that was evident even from behind, and dark hair that had grown out just long enough to curl under the edges of his helmet. Wilshire walked directly ahead of Ramsey. He had skin the color of charcoal, a British accent, and shoulders so broad they tested the fabric of his fatigues and made his backpack look like a child's. In one hand he carried the larger of Ramsey's cases; the other held a Heckler & Koch G36 assault rifle with a 40mm AG36 underbarrel grenade launcher as though it weighed no more than a feather. Moya nipped at Ramsey's heels. He was perhaps the shortest and least bulky of the men, but he radiated a kind of nervous energy that made Ramsey uncomfortable on a primal level. Moya's nose was flat, his cheekbones broad and rugged, and his lips constantly writhed over square white teeth that appeared to have been designed for a mouth far larger than his. He shifted Ramsey's other case and his rifle restlessly from one hand to the other. Grimstad brought up the rear, often vanishing into the scrub behind them and reemerging as though from a mist that clung only to him. No amount of face paint could mask his Scandinavian features or eyes so blue they were like polished spheres of amethyst. His movements were economical, and yet he looked as though he moved in jumps and starts, here and then gone, like a movie on an old reel-to-reel projector, only missing intermittent frames. They all shared one characteristic that Ramsey found more than a little unnerving.

None of them appeared to blink.

The eastern horizon was a blood-red smear through the branches, a wound inflicted upon the sky by the jagged peaks, when Rockwell slowed the exhausting pace he had set for them. Ramsey smelled the faintest traces of a campfire and spoiled meat beneath the sticky-sweet aroma of the evergreens. Wisps of smoke drifted through the canopy as they advanced. The path leveled, and for the first time Ramsey noticed several spots where the ground cover had been disturbed by footsteps. The stench of urine and feces made his stomach churn and forced him to cover his mouth and nose with his hand. A cloud of black flies buzzed from beyond the trees ahead and to his left, at the bottom of a ravine, where the bank of the stream was choppy with mud, the divots filled with standing yellow fluid. Heaps of feces as tall as termite mounds stood from the stream, its current too gentle to carry the piles away.

Rockwell stopped in his tracks, his silhouette wavering in the smoke, framed by the branches of the trees around him. He turned and Ramsey could feel the weight of his stare upon him. When Ramsey reached the man's side, he found himself at the crest of a bowl-shaped valley, at the bottom of which several fires still burned, more ember and cinder than actual flame. The smoke was trapped in the valley like a gray haze of smog, swirling and eddying around a dozen tents constructed from mismatched blankets, sheets, and tarps over irregular frameworks of boughs broken from the large pines. The grasses and shrubs had been trampled flat, scorched black in sections, and were blotched with shapes that at first appeared to be logs, for all the definition he could glean through the smoke.

A soft breeze flowed down the mountainside, blowing the smoke into his face, and, worse, a stench so powerful that it hit him in the gut like a fist.

Rotting meat.

He barely had time to identify the putrid aroma before he was vomiting into the weeds beside the path.

Ramsey wiped his lips and tried to swallow back the taste of acid in his mouth as he stared down into the valley once more.

Those weren't logs.

They were bodies, haphazardly scattered around the makeshift dwellings.

Jesus. This was why they'd brought him here.

"Welcome to North Korea, Dr. Ramsey," Rockwell said.

~*~

The smell intensified with every step down the eroded slope. Ramsey was thankful he'd already purged his stomach, but that didn't prevent the dry heaves. Like the smoke, the valley seemed to jealously hoard the stench. Ramsey fished around in his backpack and nearly cried with relief when he extricated the activated-charcoal respiratory mask, which fit tightly over his mouth and nose.

"They say all smells are particulate," Grimstad said in a thick Norwegian accent.

"So breathe through your mouth and let me know how it tastes," Wilshire said.

Ramsey tried to tune them out as he picked his way down the hillside, his vision blurred by tears, whether as a consequence of the smoke, the gut-wrenching aroma, or the sheer number of lives lost he couldn't be quite sure.

"What is this place?" he asked as they neared the bottom.

"Refugee camp," Rockwell said, his voice attenuated by his own mask. "There have to be dozens of them all along the border. These guys are like rats abandoning a sinking ship."

Tendrils of smoke drifted along the ground like the ghosts of the dead searching through the remains for their lost bodies. There had to be at least a hundred corpses, some sprawled on their backs, others on their chests or sides, but none of them appeared to have gone peacefully. If anything, it looked like they had been felled in stride, brought down in the midst of their panicked flight, most of them around the perimeter of the camp near the edge of the woods. The dirt surrounding them was scuffed, the grass uprooted, but it wasn't until he neared the first tent that he saw the copious amounts of blood and had to avert his eyes. Only then did he notice that the conversation behind him had ceased and all four soldiers held their rifles at the ready. Their eyes roved across the carnage and the far wall of trees that ringed the meadow to the north.

The bodies that had fallen into the fire pits still smoldered, their burnt black flesh split, their skin and clothing now ashes that darkened the ground like polluted snow. The majority of the tents had been saved, while a few still burned as a result of the spilled kerosene that had leeched into the soil from the scorched and crumpled canisters.

Moya fanned out to the left toward the stream, while Grimstad headed to the right. Wilshire picked his way through the killing field en route to the far side.

Ramsey turned to find Rockwell watching him. The two Pelican cases from Ramsey's lab sat beside him in the weeds.

"You know what you have to do," Rockwell said.

Ramsey tried to tell him how his project had never been tested on a human being, how it was possible that it might not even work, but when he opened his mouth, no words came out. In his mind, he was already crouched over one of the bodies, his hands and arms crusted with blood to the elbows, wishing he was back in his lab with a steaming mug of coffee, a crisp white lab coat, and a sink with running water and soap mere feet away.

Rockwell's eyes caught his, and within them Ramsey saw a flicker of disappointment, and perhaps even contempt.

"We don't have time to screw around, Dr. Ramsey. Hostilities could boil over on either side of the border at any second now and we could find ourselves right in the middle of World War Three. We need to know exactly what happened here if we're to have a prayer of averting it."

"How could anything that happened in a refugee camp in the middle of nowhere have any possible bearing on what's going on out there?" Ramsey made a sweeping gesture meant to encompass the entire region.

"It's our belief that the Democratic People's Republic of Korea is covering up something so horrible that Kim Jong-un would sooner risk wading into a war that would lead to the total annihilation of his country than allow that secret to come out." Rockwell lifted both cases, shoved the smaller of the two at Ramsey, and shouldered him into the camp toward the nearest corpse. "Look at the wounds, doctor."

Ramsey took a deep breath and stared down at the body of a young woman who couldn't have been more than twenty years old.

Her right arm was extended, her fingers curled into the soil, her left arm pinned under her chest. Her face was buried in the ground under a tangle of her dark hair, which fluttered on the breeze. An amoeba of blood had soaked into the ground around her and hardened to a cracked black crust. Her tattered clothes revealed her bruised and discolored flesh, bloated with putrefaction and crawling with black flies. There were numerous parallel lacerations so deep that the muscle and connective tissue had retracted to expose the rust-colored bone. There was a savage wound at the side of her neck, from which the meat had been ripped away. The arterial spurt from her severed carotid had painted the grass in a ten-foot crimson arc.

"Christ," Ramsey whispered. "It looks like she was attacked by an animal."

"They all do, doctor."

Ramsey glanced across the camp and saw a dozen more bodies nearby, all of which showed similar gashes. Chunks of flesh had been hacked from their bodies as if by shovels. A sensation of numbness washed over him, lending the feeling that while he was physically present, his body had somehow distanced itself from the massacre. He looked back at Rockwell to see the man's façade of patience begin to crumble.

"We need to do this now, Dr. Ramsey." He spoke through bared teeth. "How can I be of assistance to you?"

Ramsey stared into his eyes for a long moment, steeled his nerve, then set down his case and popped the latches.

"Help me roll her over, would you?"

IV

Ramsey had both cases open flat on the ground beside him, his equipment set up on the foam inserts so as not to get any blood or dirt on or in the expensive electronic components. He turned on the thousand-watt Yamaha portable compact gas-powered generator from the larger case and repeated the process for the three units plugged into it. Under ideal circumstances and normal power usage, the generator would provide roughly twelve hours of electricity before they would need to track down more fuel, which was more than enough time to do everything he needed to do many times over.

He felt a surge of excitement. This was what he had been waiting for. After all of the hours of research and experimentation, all of the years of planning and designing and building, he was finally about to find out if they had been worth it. His pulse pounded in his temples and his hands trembled. His breathing raced in anticipation. He was finally going to do it. At long last, his dreams were about to come—

And then he looked into the woman's lifeless face and the excitement was gone. He felt like the acids in his stomach were trying to eat right through him and wished he could throw up.

"We're burning daylight," Rockwell said. The black paint on his face glistened with sweat. His fatigues were blotched with blood and chunks of flesh to which strands of black hair clung. He had selected five of the most violently mutilated corpses and dragged them over to where Ramsey had set up his field lab, beside which they rested shoulder-to-shoulder on the grass, staring up into the sky as the pink dawn faded to a deep blue to the east, the stars winking out of being to the west.

The other three soldiers patrolled the perimeter, rifles seated against their shoulders, ducking in and out of the dense forest and the shadows that lurked within.

Ramsey arranged the primary electronic components beside him and withdrew a stainless steel tool of his own design. It looked like a pair of salad tongs, only shorter, sturdier, and with curved ends reminiscent of spoons. He gripped them by the handles, focused on steadying his hands, and made every conceivable effort not to look at the woman's face until the last possible second.

"All right," he said to himself. He closed his eyes and took a deep breath. When he opened them again, he looked directly into the woman's opaque eyes. "Here we go."

He aligned the tongs with the woman's right eye and used one end to pry back her upper lid and the other to retract her lower lid. Carefully, he eased the implements deeper into her socket, the curved edges following the contours of her eyeball, which bulged outward ever so slightly. Here was the most delicate part of the procedure. He needed to be exceedingly gentle so as not to clip or impinge upon the optic nerve as he gripped the eye and slowly teased it out of the orbit.

A drop of sweat rolled into his own eye, but he refused to even blink for fear of botching the job now.

In one smooth motion, he guided the eyeball out of her skull. The lids folded inward into the hollow as the nerve unspooled between them.

Rockwell groaned.

Ramsey quickly grabbed a four-by-four square of gauze and used it to hold the eyeball while he set aside the tongs. He breathed a sigh of relief.

"Could you turn her face to her left, please?"

Rockwell did as he was instructed and Ramsey rested the eye and the gauze on the now-flat surface of her right temple.

"Walk me through this as you're doing it," Rockwell said.

Ramsey gave him a curious glance.

"In case something happens to me?"

"Look around you, Dr. Ramsey."

Despite the respirator, Ramsey could still smell the remains ripening, much to the delight of the buzzing flies.

"Fair enough." He selected the first of the three components, a long cable that was already plugged into one of the USB ports on his laptop. The opposite end was equipped with what looked like a suture needle, but broader and composed of silicon. He held it up for Rockwell to see, then set about his task. "You angle this special needle like so…and insert it into the optic nerve about a quarter of an inch distal to the point where the nerve meets the eyeball. You'll feel the pressure abate as the needle passes through the outer meningeal membrane, which serves as a kind of insulation and helps accelerate the electrical impulses from the eye to the brain. Once you enter the optic nerve itself, you need to be careful not to pierce the central artery as you slide it in until the entire needle is inside the nerve and the tip is seated at the point where the nerve terminates at the optic disc." He positioned the needle and draped the length of the cord over the woman's forehead so as not to place undue tension on the needle or the nerve. "What we've essentially just done here is rerouted the visual signal from the brain to the laptop, which is running a special program I designed to interpret the incoming electrical impulses and convert them into a series of pixels, almost like the LCD monitor itself."

"And that will show us the last thing she saw before she died?"

"Not by itself. Once her heart stopped beating, all electrical activity in her body ceased."

"So how is this of any use to us? We don't know who slaughtered these people. If we're going to stop a war before it starts, then we need to know what the hell—"

"Listen. It's just like they believed in ancient times. Only this is real science, not superstition. The eyes capture the last image the subject sees before his death, only it's not a picture in an ordinary sense that you can just peer through the pupil and see, like the reflection of the killer's face. Vision is a complex process that involves photostimulation and the biological conversion of light photons into an electrical signal through the process of isomerization—"

"In English."

"You're familiar with rods and cones, right?" Ramsey waited for Rockwell to nod. "The rods are designed to perceive low light levels, but have absolutely nothing to do with color vision. That's accomplished by three different types of cones that are specialized for different wavelengths of light. Short, medium, and long. Blue, green, and red, respectively. The retina is composed of millions of these cells, collectively known as photoreceptors. When light passes through the pupil, it's focused and inverted by the lens, then projected onto these cells like a movie theater screen. They become stimulated, or 'charged,' by the various wavelengths of light. Photostimulation. Think of these rods and cones as sponges, but instead of absorbing fluid, they absorb individual units of light, or photons. Through a complex chemical process, these metaphorical sponges are essentially squeezed, and the light that pours out of them is translated into an electrical impulse that flows along the optic nerve to the visual cortex of the occipital lobe, where the brain interprets these signals as a single coherent image. It's an instantaneous process, and one obviously outside of our conscious control. The photo cells are under a constant state of stimulation as long as there's life within the body. At the moment of death, however, all electrical activity ceases. There's no more current to wring the light from the rods and cones and carry the impulses to the brain, right?" Rockwell nodded. "But death is instantaneous, and not accomplished as a series of steps. So at the point when this happens, the rods and cones are still stimulated by photons that can't be converted to electrical impulses without outside intervention. All we're doing is providing that intervention. We're converting that stored light, that potential, into one final electrical signal that we'll be able to see."

"And it's photographic quality? I mean, would there be enough detail to identify a face?"

"The image won't be perfect. Significant degradation occurs as time passes after death. It's part of the process of decomposition. In a nutshell, the stored light starts to seep out. So we need to not only amplify the light in those cells, but fill in the gaps created by dead cells, which is another function of my program. It creates a gray-scale gradient between pixels that approximates the missing shade between them."

"So the image won't be in color?"

"Oh, there will definitely be color. See this piece here?" Ramsey held up the second component, which looked like a jeweler's loupe with a suction cup for a base. An electrical cord trailed from a square box on its side. "Inside of this eyepiece is a tiny laser, which moves back and forth extremely quickly, like you would scribble with a pen, only its horizontal orientation changes slightly with each pass. This laser reenergizes the rods and cones, and essentially 'tops them off' with light, while simultaneously stimulating the conversion of the photons to negatively charged electrons, and accelerating them along their natural pathway, or, in this case, our artificial optic nerve.

"This third piece…" He showed Rockwell what looked like a solar cell the size of a playing card, then attached it to the top of the laser loupe. "…functions like an artificial retina. When the laser charges the photo cells in the subject's eye, each of them releases a small, nearly undetectable amount of visible light that this phosphor-enhanced photodetector absorbs and transmits to the laptop via this other USB cable. This image is hazy and ill-defined, but serves as an overlay for the one from the nerve itself. The two separate layers are then combined, merged, and run through a gamut of filters to produce a reasonably sharp two-dimensional snapshot of the last thing the subject would have seen at the exact moment of his death."

"You're confident that it will work?"

Ramsey hesitated.

"Like I said, I've never tested it on a human being, but we used a similar setup to produce the desired results with mice and rats. The only problem is their eyes aren't nearly as complex as ours. It's like comparing a primitive drawing on the wall of a cave to a plasma-screen television."

"But it worked, right?"

"We immobilized them in such a way that they could see a clock when they were euthanized. On the images we obtained, I could see the precise moment that each individual died. To the second."

"So get on with it already." Rockwell smiled, but there was no warmth in it. "And if it doesn't work, I'm sure you'll be able to find your own way home again, won't you?"

Ramsey pushed that thought aside and fired up the initialization sequence. The laser optics produced a high-pitched whine like a swarm of mosquitoes. He oriented the woman's brown iris to align with the center of the loupe, then affixed the suction cup to her eyeball, careful not to jostle the needle or the cord. The program on the laptop screen displayed three separate ready beacons. When all of them turned green, he glanced up at Rockwell, held his breath, and pressed the launch key.

~*~

The faintest hint of red glowed through the sclera and darkened the lightning-bolt vessels that riddled the eyeball. The laser housing vibrated in his hand. The generator rumbled in the grass.

Ramsey gnawed on his lip while he watched the laptop monitor for any sign success.

It wasn't going to work.

Every second passed as an eternity. He could feel the weight of Rockwell's stare upon him, a burden compounded by his own dawning sense of failure. After everything he had endured to place himself in this position…After all of the travails…Here he knelt, thousands of miles from home with the opportunity of a lifetime sprawled before him, only to watch his creation fail when he needed it to work the most. When people were counting on him. When the entire world was counting on him.

His eyes dampened and he batted his eyelids to stall the tears of frustration and desperation and utter crushing heartbreak. There would be no shot at redemption. No renewal of his funding. No hope for the future. He would return to his lab to find all of his possessions crammed into a box with a pink slip taped to the lid and a pair of MPs waiting to escort him from the premises. His career was over. His life was over. To come so far and ultimately fall short—

The blank screen filled with dots, like stars being birthed into the night sky.

Ramsey nearly sobbed out loud when he released the stale breath he didn't realize he was holding.

Everything happened quickly from there. The sporadic dots became many, until they filled the monitor. A ghostly gray image materialized—spectral, haunting—with no apparent pattern. It was like trying to decode the hidden message in a bank of clouds. And then the first wave of filters kicked in, one after another after another, each vertical comb sharpening the image until contrast started to emerge.

The laser stilled in his hand.

"It's working," he said.

"The picture's for shit," Rockwell said. "I can't tell what I'm supposed to be seeing."

A download bar appeared on the screen. Thirty percent complete. Sixty. Ninety. Ninety-five.

The bar vanished and the color overlay appeared as if by magic: blotches of green and blue and red, like spatters of paint flung from a brush onto the gray background. The hard drive whirred as the final wave of filters launched. One hot on the heels of the last.

"This was a total waste of our time," Rockwell said. "I told them this was a stupid plan, that my team should just press on and take matters into our own hands, not wait for some goddamn scientist with his fool computer—"

His words trailed into a silence scarred by the echoing sounds of their breathing through the masks.

"Holy Mother of God..." Rockwell whispered.

Ramsey felt the warmth of tears on his cheeks, but couldn't summon the strength to raise his arms to wipe them away. All he could do was stare at the monitor, millions of thoughts racing and colliding inside his head. He managed to grasp one that seemed to encompass every emotional and rational reaction in two little words.

"It worked."

And as he appraised the image on the screen, swelling with a sense of pride, the reality of the situation came crashing down on him.

This was the last thing the woman saw when her heart stopped beating, an image that she would never see because the part of her that had lived inside this now-lifeless vessel had already departed. This was a part of her life she would never know. And for that Ramsey was grateful. It was one small mercy bestowed upon her by an otherwise uncaring God, one split-second of terror and misery that wouldn't follow her into the afterlife. He prayed that, wherever she was, she remembered none of those immediately preceding it either, for what he saw chilled him to the marrow.

"What the fuck is that?" Rockwell said.

Ramsey could only shake his head.

In the upper right corner of the screen, the treetops were silhouetted against the night sky, the horizon slanted, the stars blurred by motion. There was a dark shape in the foreground, too close to the woman to clearly see. A wild mane of dark hair, highlighted by the glow of what Ramsey could only assume was one of the campfires that still smoldered behind him even now. The merest hint of those flames were reflected from the corner of an eye and shimmered on the scarlet fluid that coated the cheek and forehead. A burst of fluid was trapped in midair beside the face, like the first bite from an overripe orange, forever frozen in time. And in the center of the face was a clearly delineated black hole.

Rockwell tapped the monitor.

"Get me some definition right there. I need to see that face."

"I can't," Ramsey whispered.

"Hit some keys. Type some commands. Use whatever filters or masks you have. I don't care how you do it. Just get me that face!"

"I can't."

Rockwell grabbed him by the collar of his jacket and jerked him across the woman's body until their noses were scant inches apart, their respirators touching. The soldier's eyes were wide and wild.

"Get me that goddamn face!"

Ramsey dropped the eyeball and shoved Rockwell in the chest.

"It's the *punctum caecum!*" he shouted. "There's absolutely nothing I can do about it!"

Rockwell balled his fists and tensed as though about to lunge again. His cheeks were flushed and his chest heaved like a bull preparing to charge.

"It's the blindspot," Ramsey said, straightening his jacket. "Every eye has one. There are no photoreceptor cells at the point where the optic nerve enters the retina. No rods. No cones. No nothing. Just an empty space. With seamless visual stimulation, our brains just fill in that gap. But what we're looking at here is a single millisecond in time. One frame of a movie. For all intents and purposes, nothing exists within that black hole."

"Surely there's something that fancy program of yours can do to fill it in."

The effort required to maintain the pretense of patience made the veins in Rockwell's neck stand out like green worms writhing under his skin.

"No," Ramsey said. "There's nothing more I can do."

Rockwell stared at him for an interminable, uncomfortable moment.

"Then you'd better get started on the others."

With that, Rockwell shoved himself to his feet and stormed across the field littered with corpses toward the far tree line. The smoke drifted around him, making it appear as though he were burning.

Ramsey sighed and collapsed onto his haunches. Can't win for losing, right? He leaned over the computer and sent the image to the digital photo printer, which hummed for several seconds before commencing with its task.

He removed the eight-by-ten glossy from the tray and held up so he could clearly see it. The hackles rose across his shoulders and crept up his neck. His heart rate accelerated. He noticed that his hands were shaking as he peered through the eye of a dead woman into the featureless face of the monster who appeared to be tearing out her throat with its teeth.

Ramsey set the picture aside and again found his tongs. He wanted to make sure he returned the woman's eye to her socket. It seemed the only small measure of compassion he could provide for the frightened girl who had fled the potential nuclear holocaust in her country only to meet with an even more violent end. When he was through and had closed her eyelids for the final time, he glanced at the line of bodies beside her. It felt as though all of them were looking right at him, eager to unburden themselves of the horrible knowledge they had taken with them to their graves.

~*~

Two hours later, they were on the move again, the refugee camp fading into memory like the residua of a nightmare. The smoke had cleared, the stench was gone, and no longer did the buzzing drone of flies interrupt his every thought. Ramsey removed his mask and breathed in the fresh air, allowing it to linger in his chest, cleansing him from the inside out. He savored the scents of evergreen needles and pine sap and the blossoms of wildflowers and the dampness of the moss in his sinuses. These were the simple joys often taken for granted, like the gentle caress of the breeze on his sweat-dampened face and the sensation of blood pumping through his strong legs. He was even thankful for the way his feet ached in the new boots and the way the helmet scraped the crown of his head and the pain in his back from the heavy pack. All of these things, the good and the bad, the pleasurable and the painful, served to prove that he was still alive, that all was right with the world, if only for this one moment in time.

More importantly, they distracted him from the images he had seen, now captured on the photographic paper in the case Moya carried. Ramsey never wanted to see them again. It didn't matter, though. Once he had seen them, they had become a part of him, patches in the quilt of his own existence. He would carry the memories of the dead with him until the day finally arrived for him to join their ranks and expel them on his dying breath into the mist of accumulated sorrows that grew thicker in the air with each passing day. He didn't want their memories, but it was the cross he had chosen to bear, the one he had set about building years ago with the inkling of an idea and a microscope.

They had all been the same, these visions of death, variations upon a theme of pain and suffering that should by all rights have been outside the realm of human experience. Not one had been an easy death, and had he been able to capture the sounds of their passing alongside the sights, the soundtrack would have been the tormented screams of the damned. All but the last, whose final memory must have been accompanied by the sounds of tearing flesh and splattering blood.

Six people. Four men. Two women. Each of them butchered by different faceless apparitions with wild hair, light glistening on the masks of blood they wore like war paint. Some glimpsed slender fingers with filthy, hooked nails. Others caught a flash from sharp teeth, dripping with strands of saliva and blood. And still others had the misfortune of staring their deaths in the eye and seeing their painful fates reflected back at them.

Six had been enough for him. For all of them. And still they were no better off for their newfound knowledge. They didn't know exactly what attacked those poor souls any more than they knew where the enemy now lurked. All they knew with any kind of certainty was that at any minute the skies could fill with missiles and radiation and ash. And that they were isolated in the wilderness with whatever had slaughtered more than a hundred refugees with such speed and ferocity that not a single survivor had been spared.

Ramsey peered through the canopy overhead, praying for just a glimpse of the sun. He treasured the birdsong and the sounds of the needles and branches rubbing together and the shapes and colors of the leaves on the elms and the ashes. He focused on the crunching sounds of the soldiers shoving through the bushes both ahead of him and behind him, on the sounds of their breathing and their footsteps, on just the simple fact that their presence meant that he wasn't alone.

He focused on anything and everything in order to distract himself from looking down and seeing the automatic rifle he now clutched in his trembling hands.

Or the droplets of blood that had dried on the groundcover like wilted crimson flowers.

Or the fresh tracks they followed relentlessly to the northwest.

V

None of the men spoke of the nature of their quarry. They didn't have to. Their concern was written into the lines of their faces, the set of their bulging jaws, their mannerisms. A nervous energy radiated from them, like so many downed high-tension cables snapping between them. Ramsey may have been a soldier once upon a time, but he was nothing like these men. While they eagerly tracked their prey, rifles unwavering in their grasps, anticipating the seemingly inevitable confrontation, all he felt was fear. He couldn't think of a single logical reason why anyone would attack a helpless refugee camp, let alone with their bare hands and teeth. There was obviously something very wrong with the people whose passage they followed, an element of savagery and violence that could only be described as inhuman.

The individual footprints were impossible to differentiate. They were placed one on top of the other in chaotic fashion so as to obscure potential distinctions and hide their numbers. Gleaning any specific details from the bare granite, lush grasses, and spongy detritus was a hopeless proposition.

What in God's name was he still doing here? He had served his purpose. Rockwell knew how to use his equipment. They didn't need him anymore. And now that he had successfully demonstrated the capabilities of his prototype, he would never have to go looking for funding ever again. There would probably be stacks of cash waiting in his lab when he returned, enough to build a dozen new units to replace this one if he left it behind. So why didn't he just turn around now? He could follow their trail all the way back to the temple where the chopper had dropped him off what already felt like a lifetime ago. It couldn't be too hard to locate the nearest town from there, could it?

He glanced back over his shoulder. The forest appeared to be following them, swallowing their path behind them. Moya had tied the Pelican case by its handle to the pack on his back in order to free both hands for his weapon. His fingers clenched and unclenched their grip. His eyes roved from one side of the path to the other, peeling apart the branches and leaves to penetrate the lurking shadows, never once blinking. Behind him, Grimstad walked in reverse, guarding their rear with his rifle firmly seated against his shoulder. As though they expected the attack to commence at any second.

As though they sensed something that he didn't.

The prospect of striking out on his own was more terrifying than simply going with the flow. At least there was safety in numbers, he figured, and hoped the refugees hadn't felt the same way. He couldn't stomach the prospect of facing that valley of death again, especially all by himself. He only wished that Rockwell, who carried their sole means of communication, a secure satellite uplink in a case in his pack, would use it, but despite Ramsey's most well-reasoned arguments, Rockwell had refused, stating that he would only use it in case of a genuine crisis. If this wasn't one, then Ramsey sure as hell didn't want to be around for the real thing. Besides, Rockwell had said, an emergency evacuation was too risky. Sending a chopper across the border into North Korea, even one flying the U.N. flag, could be seen as an act of provocation, and could provide just the slightest nudge required to push Kim over the edge. What he didn't say, yet still made perfectly clear, was that they were expendable in the grand scheme of things. When faced with the prospect of mass casualties and global war, their lives were inconsequential. Their mission, which no one would actually clarify for Ramsey, was of the utmost importance; however, they, as a unit, were not. Only a select few in the highest places even knew they were here, and they would undoubtedly deny that knowledge should it ever come to light.

They were on their own, and they all knew it.

Billions of people were counting on them to stop a war before it started, whether they realized it or not. And if everything played out as planned, they never would.

By the same token, if they too were slaughtered like the refugees, their bodies would be left to rot in the middle of these godforsaken mountains.

Ramsey turned around again and bumped into Wilshire from behind. He hadn't seen him stop. The soldier whirled and glared at him, then quickly looked back to where Rockwell stood motionless at the side of the trail, a dozen paces ahead, staring down the barrel of his rifle into a thick copse of Mongolian oak trees.

The wind rustled the leaves overhead, and somewhere in the distance he heard the cry of a hawk.

Ramsey held his breath and waited. No one moved. What did Rockwell see?

Slowly, one cautious step at a time, Rockwell pressed silently through the tall weeds and disappeared into the forest. The seconds stretched to minutes, and Ramsey found his finger fidgeting with the trigger of his rifle. He shifted his weight, eliciting a crinkling sound from the detritus. Wilshire shot him another disapproving look.

What was Rockwell doing back there?

And then Ramsey smelled it. He had been so focused on watching and listening that he hadn't noticed the smell of feces until the wind shifted and blew it into his face. The scent was fresh, but there was something wrong with it. It was a sickly aroma that reminded him of a cross between carrion and diarrhea.

The wind shifted again and Rockwell emerged from the shivering branches. Ramsey couldn't read the expression on the soldier's painted face, but apparently the others could. They were moving before Ramsey even knew they were about to.

He followed them through the overgrowth to where Rockwell waited in the shadows of the oaks. The sunlight filtering through the leaves created kaleidoscopic patterns on his face.

Ramsey recoiled from the stench and scrambled to get his mask back out of his pack. The smell was different than the one in the clearing, but every bit as repulsive. It was how he imagined it would smell if a herd of cattle had been strung up from the boughs, gutted, and their bowels and viscera left to rot. Even the mask barely attenuated the vile aroma that seemed to have found its way inside his nostrils, where it promptly curled up, died, and began to rapidly decompose.

None of the men spoke. Instead, they communicated with glances, as only men who were privy to each other's every waking thought could. Despite his recent arrival, it didn't take Ramsey long to catch up. The detritus was spattered with loose stool. As were the leaves of the lower canopy, the trunks of the trees, and the shrubs surrounding them. It looked like a cross between oil and tar had been dumped from the sky. And Ramsey knew exactly what caused stool to blacken.

Blood.

The spoor was black and runny because it consisted of little more than straight blood.

But how had it ended up spattered across just about every available surface?

Ramsey swatted the swirling cloud of bloated black flies away from his face and followed the eyes of the other men up into the trees, to a point roughly twenty feet above them, where the bark had been scraped from a thick branch the width of his calf. The exposed wood beneath was gouged with parallel gashes, the edges crusted with sap. Nearly every one of the branches up there was similarly scarred. At first, Ramsey was reminded of what deer and elk did to pine trees with their antlers, but those markings were much closer to the ground, not where the only way to reach them was with an extension ladder.

He flashed back to the similar wounds on the bodies in the clearing and shivered at the thought.

Wilshire knelt beside a particularly foul puddle, dabbed his fingertip into it, and rubbed it against the pad of his thumb.

"Less than twenty-four hours old," he whispered.

"They spent the night in the trees?" Grimstad said.

"No," Wilshire said, wiping his fingers on the ground. "Not the night. The day. I suspect they're moving under the cover of darkness."

"Which means that they have an eight hour lead on us," Rockwell said. "At the most."

"Where are we in relation to the site of the detonation?" Grimstad said.

"Sixteen kilometers north-northwest of here," Moya said.

Ramsey finally made the connection.

"Then if we follow our current course, the trail should lead us straight to it."

"See?" Moya said. "I told you it would be useful having a college boy around. We never would have figured that out otherwise."

"Stow it," Rockwell said. "He's the only reason we have the slightest idea of what we're dealing with here."

"If we push it, we can be there before nightfall," Wilshire said.

Ramsey glanced up through the shivering leaves, hoping for a glimpse of the sun, but instead saw only dark shadows with wild hair clinging to the branches, claws buried in the wood. He understood the implications. Unless the tracks they were following veered in a different direction, they would potentially overtake their quarry before sunset.

His grip grew slick on his rifle.

A stray thought forced its way to the forefront of his mind. Was there a relationship between the detonation and the vicious marauders they now followed? Based on the timing, it had to be more than mere coincidence.

Ramsey lowered his eyes and caught Rockwell's stare. Within it, he saw something more closely resembling recognition than confusion, knowledge as opposed to curiosity.

What did he know?

This was all wrong. He had been summoned from Ft. Detrick after these men had already discovered what happened in the refugee camp. They were witnesses to the fact that the people had been attacked by tooth and nail. He understood now. They hadn't needed Ramsey to figure out what had happened, but rather to show them the face of an enemy they already knew existed, to confirm whatever suspicions they already had.

They knew. They had known all along.

"Tell me what's out there?" Ramsey said, stepping into Rockwell's personal space. "Whose tracks are we following and what kind of trap are we walking into?"

Rockwell cocked his head, almost as a predatory bird might, and appraised him with a smirk on his face.

"Saddle up, doctor," he finally said. "We have a long walk ahead of us."

And with that, he turned and strode back through the bushes, leaving Ramsey standing in the wretched copse of oaks, wondering what in God's name he had been volunteered for and if anyone had ever expected him to make the return trip.

An overwhelming sense of isolation settled over him and he threw himself through the underbrush to catch up with the others.

~*~

They smelled the smoke long before they saw it; a black smudge that diffused the afternoon sun over the sharp crest of the next ridge. It took more than an hour and a half to pick their way over the steep incline to a point where they could slide down the loose granite and scree, slaloming between rugged escarpments and the trunks of trees that rooted themselves to the windswept terra by spite alone, until they reached the bottom of the valley, where a crystalline lake sparkled through the forest. The first thing they saw was the reflection from the hood of a jeep...and then the body sprawled across it.

A haze of gun smoke clung to the evergreen canopy like smog, an entirely pleasant smell compared to the coppery biological scent that grew stronger with every step. It wasn't the cloying stench of decomposition. Not yet, anyway. Soon enough it would turn, as the gasses swelled and the fluids settled, but for now, the mere scent of blood freed from its vessels was easily enough filtered by their respirators.

They emerged cautiously from the tree line onto the terminus of a rutted track that might once have qualified as a road, but from which now grew waist-high weeds and brambles. Wilshire used a pair of shears to snip the barbed wire fence on the opposite side, which featured rusted warning signs written in Korean every thirty feet. The only symbol Ramsey recognized was a fairly self-explanatory skull-and-crossbones that would have served as a reasonably effective deterrent under normal circumstances, but even more so now that its promise was clearly fulfilled at the far end of the clearing before them. Three olive-green Jeeps were parked just beyond the edge of the field, the grasses obscuring their grills, their headlights still shining. The overhanging branches did their best to hide their windshields. The Jeep closest to the lake to the north looked as though it had tried to make a break from cover, only to strike a tree trunk with its crumpled right front quarter-panel and send its driver straight through the glass and onto the hood, where carrion birds squabbled over the mess they had made of the man's neck and shoulders. His hands were plucked of flesh to the bones.

The big brown vultures stared them down as they approached, then, unperturbed, resumed their meal. Grimstad hurled a rock into their midst and sent them squawking and squalling into the trees, where they watched from the shadowed enclaves, occasionally shrieking their indignation.

The rest of the bodies were scattered throughout the forest to the east and all the way into the standing water in the reeds bordering the lake. There had to be at least twenty of them, all sprawled on the scuffed detritus, their automatic rifles either still in their hands or within close reach. The surrounding trunks were riddled with bullet holes from which ribbons of sticky sap still bled. They all wore woodland camouflage-patterned CBRN suits made from charcoal-lined Demron, designed to protect them from any chemical, biological, radiological, or nuclear hazard they could possibly encounter, with black overboots and elaborate gas masks with full face shields.

Moya rolled one of the men onto his side and revealed the red and blue-striped insignia emblazoned on the breast.

"Korean People's Army," he said. "They're North Korean."

"Trying to clean up their own mess," Wilshire said.

"Doesn't look like they did an especially good job, does it?" Moya chuckled. "And here we were worried about running into resistance."

"They know these men are dead," Rockwell said. "It's only a matter of time before they dispatch more, if they haven't already."

"I'm surprised there aren't planes circling overhead," Grimstad said. "They could easily just napalm the whole area and be done with it."

"The moment the South Koreans pick up fighter planes streaking across the radar into the demilitarized zone and toward their border, they'll launch their own counter-attack. And with the Chinese poised to drop the hammer and sickle on them from the north, a highly visible offensive has to be considered a last resort. Any deployment would have to be essentially invisible."

"So you think they'll just keep sending unit after unit to be slaughtered?" Wilshire said. "They don't have a whole lot of time left to handle this quietly before someone out there gets tired of the posturing and all hell breaks loose. Especially considering Beijing has to realize this only accelerates its timetable by a few years at the most. This could prove to be an ideal time to strike, while there's still a chance the Chinese can be perceived as a victim in all of this."

"Then we're wasting our time debating this," Rockwell snapped. "We know the North Koreans will be sending more troops, and in greater numbers, and we sure as Christ don't want to be here when they arrive. This is up to us from here and we're already out of time."

Ramsey listened to them talk while he wandered through the forest, scrutinizing the remains, trying to distance himself from the terror that threatened to overwhelm him. Let the others forget he was here. The more they talked, the more they unintentionally shared with him. Unfortunately, there were still crucial gaps in his knowledge. What were the North Koreans hiding that was worth risking their utter destruction to protect, and what was its relationship to whatever was out here in these mountains massacring everyone in its path?

He crouched and peered through the cracked visor over a dead soldier's face. The man was propped against the trunk of an alder, his legs spread before him. He held the rifle in his lifeless hand by the barrel, its butt crusted with blood where he had used it as a club when the last of his ammunition was gone. Like the others around him, he appeared to have put up a valiant fight against an enemy that had simply been too strong. His suit was in tatters, the exposed skin bloody and raw. Rust-colored droplets speckled the inside of his mask, and his head leaned sharply to his right, only partially concealing the fact that half of his neck and been torn away. Ramsey used a stick to tip the man's head and saw severed tendons and the knobs of the cervical spine, all crawling with insects that weren't about to fly away and abandon the meal of a lifetime.

"You know what you need to do," Rockwell said from behind him.

Ramsey jerked the stick back so quickly that the man's head nearly toppled from his shoulders. He turned just as Rockwell dropped both of the Pelican cases onto the ground and felt a surge of anger. He wasn't their trained monkey. It was high time they gave him some answers.

"What will that accomplish?" he said, his voice rising. "It sounds like you guys already know what's going on here. So let's just skip the song and dance and get right down to it."

"Just do your goddamn job, doctor."

Rockwell turned away from Ramsey and started back toward where the others were gathered, now conspiring in whispers.

"No," Ramsey said. The word tumbled out of his mouth before he had the chance to think it through.

Rockwell stopped dead in his tracks and stood perfectly still, as though running through his memory to confirm that he had actually heard what he thought he had.

Ramsey screwed up his courage and forged on. In for a penny, in for a pound and all that.

"Not until you tell me exactly what we're doing here. You know what's out here killing all of these people, don't you? If you expect me to risk my life out here with you, then you'd better tell me right now what—"

Rockwell rounded on him so quickly that Ramsey never even saw it coming. He was lifted from his feet by his jacket and slammed against the tree, knocking the dead man onto the ground.

"Now you listen to me," Rockwell snarled. "I'm in command out here. I determine what you need to know and what you don't. Right now, all I need you to do is perform the one simple function that you were brought here to perform, and I expect you to do so at this very moment without contradicting a direct order from the only man out here who gives a rat's ass whether you make it back to the 'States alive or not."

He shoved Ramsey against the trunk for emphasis and then released him.

Ramsey fell to the dirt and pushed himself right back to his feet.

"Not until you tell me what I want to know."

Rockwell laughed, but there was no humor in it. His face reddened and his eyes narrowed to slits.

"Don't forget you already showed me how to use your equipment, doctor. You don't have as much leverage as you obviously think you do."

"You think I'm stupid?" Ramsey brushed off the knees of his pants. "The computer program is password-protected and I never showed you the proper initialization sequence."

"You said you were going to show me everything."

"I lied."

Rockwell appraised him for nearly a full minute. Ramsey refused to crack under the intense scrutiny.

"You're bluffing."

"Try me."

Rockwell's jaw muscles bulged as they clenched and unclenched, his stare boring straight through Ramsey, who was on the verge of caving in when Rockwell finally spoke.

"In November of 2010, the U.N. Security Council dispatched an envoy, headed by an American nuclear scientist named Siegfried Hecker, to tour what was supposedly the only nuclear facility in the country. During that visit, Dr. Hecker observed more than two thousand specialized centrifuges at the Yongbyon site, which until mere months prior had been used as a fuel rod fabrication plant. It was Hecker's assertion, and one supported by the Security Council, that despite claims by North Korean officials that they only produced low-yield uranium for non-military purposes, the plant was fully capable of enriching enough weapons-grade uranium for two missiles annually. A subsequent investigation determined that the Yongbyon plant was merely the visible face of the North Korean nuclear program, and a small part of a much broader network. Additional intelligence provided us with nearly a dozen manufacturing and assembly sites. Of those, more than half turned out to be actively producing nuclear material, a handful were used exclusively for the construction and assembly of the various delivery systems, and the remainder, while located in the most remote locations and heavily guarded around the clock, didn't appear to have anything at all to do with the nuclear program. The only thing we could determine with our limited surveillance capabilities was that panel trucks carrying caged animals and shackled prisoners arrived routinely after sundown, and an incinerator churned ash into the sky, day and night."

"Biological experimentation? They were circumventing the Geneva Convention."

"All we could confirm was that the ashes were biological in origin, not which species they came from. We were, however, able to conclusively determine from samples of the nearby soil, air, and water that there were no traces of nuclear byproducts. What we did find were a multitude of toxins, various alkylating agents, and polycyclic aromatic hydrocarbons."

"Those are mutagens. They had to be attempting some kind of genetic manipulation."

"Exactly. So when we isolated the location of the nuclear detonation and found that it was at a site that we not only knew wasn't part of their nuclear program, but was instead at a facility we suspected was actively subjecting humans and animals to an unknown battery of mutagenic agents, we could only assume that—"

"They destroyed the facility themselves. To cover up whatever must have gone wrong."

"Or to kill whatever creation might have gotten out of control." Rockwell rubbed his bloodshot eyes. "Which, based on what we've seen so far, appears to be the case. Only they obviously didn't accomplish their goal."

"That's why you needed me. Because when you encountered the massacre at the refugee camp, you realized that something was out there, but you had no idea what it was or what it looked like."

"We still don't. All we have are pictures of dark silhouettes with little definition. So, if you're happy now, how about you see if you can get us something a little better to go on?"

Ramsey nodded.

Rockwell started back toward the others.

"And when we find them?" Ramsey said. "What then?"

"We do the job right and avert a global catastrophe in the process."

"Do the job right?"

"Boom," Rockwell said, barely loud enough to be heard. He was nearly to the others when he stopped and turned around. "I'm going to need your password and the initialization sequence. Just in case."

"Password? I don't know what you're talking about. All you have to do is turn the computer on," Ramsey said, opening the smaller case.

For the first time since they had met, Ramsey thought he saw the hint of a genuine smile tug at the corner of Rockwell's lips.

VI

Ramsey was getting faster and more adept at the procedure with every subject. In less than an hour, he had produced the final images from the retinas of four of the North Korean soldiers. Unfortunately, they were little better than the ones he had gleaned from the refugees. There were more wild-haired shadows, but, again, the killers were too close to their victims to clearly demonstrate any significant details. It was almost like they were somehow aware of Ramsey's posthumous efforts, as though they refused to be captured, even in the stare of their prey. More likely, though, they were simply too fast, capable of overcoming their victims and dispatching them with exceptional speed and efficiency, a fact corroborated by the evidence before Ramsey: An entire elite unit of soldiers had been slaughtered without taking a single one of their assailants with them.

There was another option they were reluctant to entertain. Worse than the prospect of dealing with a lightning-fast enemy was the distinct possibility that these men had simply been overwhelmed by vastly superior numbers. And considering there were only five of them...

While Ramsey had been performing his task, the others had fanned out through the impromptu battlefield in search of any clues as to what had actually transpired. They had hoped that one of the killers had been mortally wounded and just crawled off somewhere to die, but all they found were more scuffed tracks in the dirt, which offered no answers by themselves. They were simply indistinct footprints, like those they had been following all afternoon in a single-file line meant to obfuscate their numbers, suggesting a level of cunning and intelligence confirmed by the aftermath of the attack.

It was Moya who first climbed up into the trees, where he found nearly every broad branch scraped and gouged and sticky with sap. It had been an ambush. The soldiers had been lured from their Jeeps into the denser forest and under the boughs where the predators were waiting to descend from above. By the time the soldiers recognized the trap, it was already too late.

Ramsey tried not to think about their trek so far, about how many tall trees they had walked under without so much as glancing up. Had they come within mere feet of the death lurking above their heads? Had predatory eyes followed their progress from behind branches covered with leaves or needles? Were they being hunted at this very moment?

They all changed into their own camouflaged CBRN protective suits, which served to lighten their packs considerably, but made the temperature seem to skyrocket. Ramsey felt like he was slowly being roasted alive. There were worse things, he knew. As they neared the site of the detonation, they could find themselves subjected to levels of radiation so high that their skin could burn and blister. Or worse. No one had any idea how well-contained the blast might have been. The preliminary assessment of the seismic data suggested that the force of the blast had been directed downward, into the earth, and that there had been at least some degree of lateral containment, but that meant little in the grand scheme of things. Just because the radiation monitors they all wore currently showed no indication of activity didn't mean that wouldn't change from one breath to the next.

"What do we know?" Rockwell said as they struck off, again toward the northwest. His voice sounded tinny and hollow thanks to the gas mask, which was significantly more unwieldy than the lightweight respirator.

This time Moya assumed the point. He made no secret of his eagerness to use his rifle.

"They hunt at night," Wilshire said from behind Ramsey. "Or at least they have so far."

"They're agile," Grimstad said. "They can move through the trees like primates."

"And yet favor bipedal locomotion on the ground when traveling over longer distances."

"They hunt as a pack. And not just for sport. They consume their prey, as their spoor attests."

"But not in its entirety. They've left nearly intact bodies everywhere in their wake."

"So why didn't they take the bodies with them?" Rockwell said. "Why leave them to rot?"

"Could be they have every intention of going back for them," Wilshire said.

"There's no proof that they didn't take any of the bodies with them," Grimstad said. "All we have to go on is what they left behind."

"If that were the case, then we should have found some evidence near where they bedded down in the trees. Bones, hair, clothing, something. But all we found was their excrement."

"And it was so runny that either there was little of any real substance to it, or their meals didn't agree with them."

"Korean food will do that to you," Moya called back over his shoulder.

The men chuckled.

"There's another option," Ramsey said. "It's possible they're merely acting on some kind of biological impetus, seeking certain nutrients versus sating their hunger. Or maybe the killing is instinctive and their digestive systems simply can't process such large quantities of blood."

"So we're moving on to speculation, then," Rockwell said.

"They're some sort of genetically-altered people," Wilshire said.

"Or animals," Grimstad said.

"Look closely at those pictures. They're definitely people."

"Not necessarily. All you can see are blurred shadows. And considering they hunt from the trees, and use their claws and teeth as weapons, we can't afford to rule anything out at this point."

"We need better pictures."

"I can only work with what's there," Ramsey said.

"They hunt by night and sleep by day," Grimstad said.

"There's no proof to support that," Wilshire said. "And even if there were, it would be a mistake to presume that couldn't change under different circumstances. That's just been their pattern so far."

"We're speculating now. And there's plenty of proof that both groups we've encountered so far were killed at night."

"You're right. *If* we can trust the pictures. But there's no denying that the refugees were killed at least a full day prior to the soldiers and whatever killed them bedded down in that grove sometime in between, chronologically speaking."

"Which means we know which direction they're traveling."

"But why would they want to go back to the point where we believe they started?"

"Establishing their range?"

"Following the game like any other pack of predators?"

"Maybe we're assigning them too much cognitive ability," Rockwell said. "They could merely be roaming and following signs of prey. If they're animals, or even part animal, then they could be simply allowing themselves to be guided by instinct."

"Or the stars or the cycle of the moon," Grimstad said.

"It would be foolish to assume that they don't have the capacity for higher thought," Ramsey said. "The last thing we want to do is underestimate them. We need to be prepared for the fact that they could be every bit as smart as we are. If not more so. We need to consider the option that they know we're here and they're leading us into some kind of trap, just like they did with the North Korean soldiers. I mean, if they can move through the trees, why leave any tracks at all, let alone a trail so easy to follow. And why go to the trouble of hiding their numbers unless they know someone is tracking them and they want to maintain an element of surprise?"

"So you're suggesting that the slaughter of hundreds of refugees and a full battalion of soldiers was meant just to lure the five of us into a trap when it's readily apparent that they have the ability to take us down any time they want?" Rockwell said.

Moya sniggered ahead of them.

"You're missing my point," Ramsey said. "Whether they know that we, specifically, are here or not, they recognized the fact that someone would be coming after them. That implies at least a modicum of intelligence. And they were able to plan their assaults on the two groups in such a way so as not to take a single casualty of their own. All I'm saying is that we need to approach this situation as though they're smarter than we are, better prepared than we are, and hope that we're wrong."

"I guess we'll find out soon enough," Moya said.

He'd stopped on the path ahead of them and stood in a spot where the canopy opened up enough to allow the sunlight to stream through. The gold had darkened to orange and stretched Moya's shadow away from him into the underbrush. The silhouetted shapes of birds streaked past high overhead against the deep blue sky, against which a cloud of dust swelled like a bank of thunderheads.

Ramsey shivered despite the sweltering protective suit.

None of them spoke or moved for several minutes. The jagged peaks along the western horizon appeared poised to pierce the belly of the setting sun.

"*Carpe noctem*," Moya said, and headed deeper into the forest. The others followed him into the shade once more.

Ramsey cast a final glance back at the sun and prayed that he would be witness to its rebirth.

~*~

He was acutely aware of the deepening shadows. Whether the arrival of darkness signaled the commencement of the impending attack or not, he could feel the potential for violence in the air all around him; a positively electric sensation that raised the goose bumps on his body and made his nerve endings sing. No longer did birds call from the upper canopy or unseen animals cavort in the branches. Nothing scampered through the forest just out of sight. The only sounds were the muffled crunching of their footsteps on the detritus and the occasional slap of a branch whipping back from one man's passage to strike the next in line. The sky overhead grew smoky at first, then metamorphosed into a shroud of dust that filtered through the trees and powdered every surface like dirty talcum. It coated the leaves and the branches and the trunks and accumulated on their heads and shoulders. The footprints they had been following vanished beneath the dust, leaving them to navigate the trail based solely on the gaps between the bushes and trunks and the trampled weeds that marked their slaloming route. Ramsey could even taste dirt on his tongue, despite the numerous filtration canisters hooked to his mask, the visor of which he had begun to have to clear with a swipe of his hand more and more frequently.

They were closing in on Ground Zero.

All conversation had ceased and an aura of tension radiated from each of them. Regardless of the International Data Centre's repeated assurances that the computer-plotted nature of the explosion suggested subterranean detonation with maximum radiation containment, they had all taken to checking their personal dosimeters with increasing frequency. Thus far, they had registered nothing above normal background radiation levels, and the occasional sweep of the portable radiacmeter demonstrated the same, but they all knew that at any second they could wander into an invisible pocket that could seriously test the capabilities of their suits. Add to that the fact that the sun was now a fading red stain in the dust above them, and Ramsey was just about ready to crawl right out of his skin. He could barely see Rockwell's outline ahead of him and Wilshire moved like a specter through the dust behind him. Moya and Grimstad had nearly vanished altogether. Only occasionally did one of them appear before disappearing just as quickly again.

Ramsey constantly stumbled as he had begun watching the trees above him more carefully than the ground underfoot. He had no doubt that when they came, they would descend from the canopy. And he was certain that it was only a matter of time before they sprung whatever trap awaited them.

He slipped his index finger in and out of the trigger guard, making sure that the glove passed through smoothly without catching or snagging. He had already checked and rechecked the clip so many times that he was starting to worry that he might have disrupted its seating and the first casing wouldn't fire. It was all he could do to resist yanking it out, running his thumb over the brass, and slapping it home again.

And for the life of him, Ramsey couldn't figure out why in the hell he was still here. With all of the dust, he could merely slip off the side of the path and duck behind a shrub. By the time anyone noticed he was gone, he could be miles away, sprinting for everything he was worth. But the fact remained that they didn't know where the predators were. They could still be somewhere ahead of them or they could have walked right past them without even realizing it. Granted, a part of him was terrified of striking off on his own and facing the unknown, but no less so than continuing along the path and walking right into the jaws of a trap. Neither option held the slightest appeal. It all boiled down to one thing. Perhaps he felt he had something to prove to these men, to show them that despite the last decade spent in school and in various safe labs away from the front lines, he was still the soldier who had faced down heavy fire to jerry-rig the fried generator that powered the perimeter lights of their camp outside Kabul, or shimmied through underground warrens teeming with insurgents to lay fiber optic cables for surveillance.

Or maybe he had something to prove to himself.

Who was he kidding? It was hard enough putting one foot in front of another in the midst of a heavily armed Special Ops unit composed of the best soldiers not just in the country, but in the entire world. On his own, he'd last about as long as a snow cone in the Sahara and he knew it, especially if—

A crashing sound ahead of him.

Moya bellowed.

The prattle of automatic gunfire.

Tap. Tap-tap-tap. Tap.

What in the name of God was going—?

"Move!" Wilshire shouted, shoving him from behind.

Thrashing from the underbrush.

Snapping branches.

Ramsey scrambled forward, swept along on the human tide. The men beside him were little more than shadows in the swirling dust.

"What's happen—?" he started, but he was shushed from one side and elbowed from the other.

They stood perfectly still, listening to the rustling branches as they slowly fell back into place and welcomed the silence in their stead. The other men were breathing so softly that he couldn't hear their exhalations through their masks.

The men eased into a triangular formation around him, their backs to one another, the silhouettes of their rifles moving smoothly across the forest.

Minutes passed as the sun faded from the sky and darkness encroached like an entity granted form by the haze.

A clicking sound behind him.

Ramsey turned and saw a pale scarlet aura bloom from Grimstad's rifle and the thin beam of a laser streak off into the woods. Rockwell and Wilshire did the same, their laser sights slicing through the smoke and dust. It took Ramsey several moments, but he eventually found the switch for his under the barrel. They produced little actual illumination, but it was far better than nothing.

As if in response to some unspoken cue, the men silently fanned out and again advanced along the path.

Ramsey's heart was beating so loudly in his ears that he feared the others might hear it.

The forest had grown unnaturally quiet. Even the wind, it seemed, held its breath. The accumulated dust and ash muffled their footsteps. The sun slunk cowardly behind the western peaks, abandoning them to their fates. Their lasers lanced through the settling dust without providing any real light by which to survey their surroundings. Ramsey wished they had night vision goggles, but realized they wouldn't work with the gas masks anyway.

"Moya?" Rockwell whispered from ahead of him.

Ramsey watched the soldier's beam sweep across the forest to the left, then stop suddenly, focusing downward on the forest floor. Moldering leaves and weeds showed through the disturbed mat of dust. A broad-leaved shrub had shed its gray coat. There were broken and bent branches, clumps of bark scraped from the surrounding tree trunks, and what looked like a puddle of oil that responded to the red beam by turning a brilliant crimson.

"Bloody hell," Wilshire whispered.

Rockwell raised his beam from the ground to the trunk of a red pine tree. A long arterial spatter dripped slowly down the bark, channeling between the sections and around the small branches. Rockwell eased closer and slowly angled his beam up into the canopy. Ramsey followed its ascent with his eyes—

Plat.

He flinched as something wet struck his mask and hurriedly wiped it away, leaving a smudge that responded to the light from the lasers by brightening in the same fashion as the droplets overhead, clinging to the undersides of the branches and leaves. Several more droplets fell from above and pattered the detritus as he watched.

Wilshire's beam joined Rockwell's in an attempt to peel apart the darkness, searching for any sign of movement through the overlapping canopy.

Ramsey thought of the Jeeps driven right up to the edge of the forest and the bodies of the North Korean soldiers scattered throughout the dense grove. They had been lured from the relative safety of their vehicles and had elected to fan out, effectively isolating themselves from their own numbers.

"There," Grimstad whispered. His beam highlighted scarlet droplets along the path and on the shrubs beside it. He moved his laser sight through the trees as he started down the trail.

"No," Ramsey said, grabbing him by the sleeve.

Grimstad whirled with an expression on his face that Ramsey hoped he would never see again, especially directed at him.

"Let go of me or so help me—"

"He's right," Rockwell whispered. "We stay together and keep off the path. We're being baited. From here on out, everything we do needs to contain an element of unpredictability."

Grimstad acquiesced with a nod, but his anger still pulsed from him in waves.

"You'll get your chance," Rockwell whispered.

"We'll all get our chance," Wilshire echoed.

That was exactly what Ramsey most feared as he followed Rockwell away from the trail and deeper into the claustrophobic woods

VII

Straying from the beaten path into the lush underbrush made it far more difficult to mask the sounds of their passage, but considering their hidden enemy already knew they were here, it was only a matter of being able to hear their approach over the whisper of leaves and branches against their thighs and chests. To Ramsey, they sounded like a herd of stampeding elephants. He feared they wouldn't be able to detect the subtle noises of the branches scraping or nails clattering in the canopy until it was too late. As it turned out, his concerns were misplaced, for they heard the gentle dripping sounds from nearly a dozen paces away.

Moya's body was folded backward over the bough of a pine tree like a roll of carpet. Drops of blood swelled from his gloved fingertips and dripped from syrupy ribbons that wended out through the straight tears in the fabric of his hood and his broken face shield, splattering wetly onto the mat of dead leaves and dirt five feet down.

"Cover me," Rockwell whispered.

He crawled cautiously to the base of the trunk, then stood and grabbed Moya by the dangling wrists. In one swift motion, he hauled the soldier down and stepped out of the way. Moya's body crumpled to the ground with the sound of bones grinding together like broken glass. Rockwell dragged him away from the tree and back to where the others waited, scouring the forest down the barrels of their rifles.

Ramsey saw no sign of movement, but his skin prickled under the weight of unseen eyes.

A distant skritching sound.

"We need to keep moving," Grimstad whispered.

"I know, damn it," Rockwell snapped. He knelt over Moya's body and reached through the shattered remains of the dead man's mask. Ramsey caught a glimpse of the blood dribbling from the corners of Moya's mouth and coiling around his thick neck. "I just need a second."

Ramsey heard a soft sucking sound and barely had time to wonder what Rockwell was doing before his hand emerged, his fingers slick with blood. The optic nerve trailed from his closed fist. Ramsey had to look away.

Wilshire crouched over Moya's backpack a dozen paces away and opened the main pouch. He rummaged around inside until he found a large silver canister shaped like a bullet and quickly stuffed it into his own rucksack.

The skritching sound grew louder, more insistent.

Ramsey scanned the path and the surrounding shrubs for any sign of his—

There.

The smaller of the two Pelican cases had broken at the hinges, the foam inserts popped out onto the forest floor. He scrambled over and tried to close it again, but the whole case fell apart, scattering the critical electronic pieces.

"There's no time," Rockwell whispered.

Ramsey gathered the components as fast as he could and shoved them into his backpack. Replacing the generator, wherever it was, would be easy enough, but the delicate instrumentation was another matter entirely.

He leapt to his feet and caught the hint of motion from the corner of his eye.

"Go!" Grimstad shouted, shoving him from behind. "They're coming!"

Ramsey had just broken into a sprint when he heard a scratching sound and glanced back to see the branches high above him shaking as though at the behest of a violent wind.

Wilshire whirled in front of him and raised his rifle. The laser beam hit Ramsey right between the eyes. He ducked just as the golden discharge erupted from the barrel and bullets streaked past his head. The report was deafening. Someone grabbed him by the backpack and pushed him. Beneath the racket of automatic gunfire and the horrible ringing in his ears, he heard Wilshire bellowing and Grimstad shouting for them to run.

The ground teetered beneath him as the ringing in his ears wreaked havoc on his equilibrium. He stumbled from side to side, barely managing to stay on his feet. All was chaos around him. Leaves and weeds swatted at his face. Muzzles flared around him like birthing stars. The *ratta-tat-tat* of the H&Ks sounded far away, like crowds clapping from the bottom of so many wells.

He tripped and fell, but scrambled back to his feet. The ringing faded to a whine and the ground made an effort to hold still. He finally got a solid grip on his rifle and swung it backward as he crashed through the shrubs, taking aim as best he could.

The trees were positively alive with shadowed forms, ducking and dodging and lunging and leaping in dark blurs as the leaves and bark were shredded by bullets all around them. They moved with such speed and agility that it was impossible to tell how many of them there actually were. They flowed through the canopy like a tsunami, preparing to crash down on their heads.

Ramsey shouted and squeezed the trigger, sending a fusillade of bullets into the trees. The rifle nearly bucked from his grasp and the laser light climbed nearly straight up before he steadied the weapon. He couldn't clearly see the other soldiers, only the sporadic flashes of muzzle flare through the shrubs. The rifle chattered as he strafed the trees, then spun around and sprinted for everything he was worth.

A flash ahead of him as Rockwell fired directly over his head.

Ramsey ducked and hurled himself through a wall of scrub oak. He barely caught a reflection from the metal in time to keep from tangling himself in the barbed wire. A twelve-foot hurricane fence had fallen to the ground in front of him, thrusting the coiled wire on top of it forward like a razor-honed fist. There were sections where it still stood upright, others where it was completely flattened as a result of the fissures that had opened in the earth beneath it. They struck outward across the barren dirt field from the center of a haze of dust so thick that it appeared to be a solid columnar structure adjoining the heavens.

A guard tower had collapsed onto the fence to Ramsey's right and impaled itself upon its own broken stilts. Shattered glass from its spotlight sparkled on the ground amid shingles and wooden debris.

Ramsey ran toward it and crawled up onto its side, where he braced his feet, turned back to face the forest, and seated his rifle firmly against his shoulder.

The old instincts kicked in on a surge of adrenaline.

Rockwell emerged from the tree line at a sprint with Wilshire right behind him.

Ramsey squeezed the trigger and leaves and needles flew from the canopy. The men scurried up beside him as Grimstad burst from a cluster of scrub oak, firing blindly back over his shoulder. There was a ferocious crashing sound behind him like a semi truck careening through the forest.

"Go!" Grimstad shouted.

The darkness came to life behind him.

"Jesus Christ," Ramsey whispered as his carbine whirred uselessly, his magazine empty.

Ramsey turned, leaped down from the side of the shack, and hit the ground running. In his mind, he saw bodies composed of shadows flying out of the upper reaches of the trees, arms extended through the tattered foliage, legs tensed beneath them in anticipation of absorbing the impact to come and using it to propel them forward with even greater momentum. Even were he able to get into his backpack, he would lose crucial seconds searching for a spare magazine for his rifle, seconds he knew he was going to need. He could hear the rumble of footsteps behind him, feel the vibrations through his legs.

Grimstad yelled behind him and gunfire crackled.

Ramsey couldn't bring himself to so much as glance back. His movements felt sluggish, hampered by the heavy overboots and the floppy suit. His rapid breaths echoed like he was blowing into a coffee can. The dust swallowed Rockwell and Wilshire ahead of him, growing so thick that he could barely see their silhouettes, and then nothing at all.

Grimstad's shouts turned to screams and the prattle of the rifle abruptly ceased.

A hazy rectangular shape appeared through the dust, wavering like a mirage at first as the swirling dust attempted to reclaim it. The ground slanted downward toward it. It looked like the entire area had dropped a dozen feet beneath its former level. He leapt over sharp crags and crevices, over toppled tree trunks and jaggedly fractured chunks of asphalt and concrete, toward the misshapen warehouse. Its eastern half had fallen, the roof jutting upward, while the western half appeared to have slid at an angle into the earth, its second story barely above the crater. Its windows were shattered, the frames crumpled, billowing dust as though gasping for air.

This was where the nightmare had begun.

Ground Zero.

A clanging sound ahead and to his right.

Rockwell was ascending a slanted set of iron stairs toward a dark trapezoid, the door that had once sealed it warped and clinging to the rail on the landing.

Ramsey veered in that direction, crunching over broken glass and the fragmented remains of the building's apron. He saw a corpse burned to such a degree that it had blackened and curled into fetal position, its skeletal jaws opened wide enough to swallow a softball. Muzzle flare strobed and he felt bullets streaking over his head as he reached the steps and hauled himself upward. The entire staircase shook and shuddered and threatened to pry loose from its moorings, which shrieked with the sound of shearing metal.

Bullets ricocheted from the stairs behind him. He lunged for the landing and crawled under Rockwell's line of fire. Wilshire reached for him from inside the ruined doorway and dragged him through, into the darkness. He could barely see the outline of a catwalk ahead of him, canted to the left toward the main warehouse floor, a massive pit with upturned concrete jaws into which the majority of the roof had collapsed, dragging broken crates and forklifts and even what appeared to be a panel truck with it. Crisp bodies peppered the entire area like the carcasses of so many ants fried under a magnifying glass.

Ramsey pushed himself to his feet. The catwalk swayed precariously over the pitfall. A section of the railing wobbled and then fell, hitting the ground seconds later with a resounding clang. His footsteps echoed as he ran toward the closed door of a cantilevered room that must have once served as some sort of supervisory office, suspended above the warehouse floor. He reached the lone door with Wilshire right behind him and seized the knob.

It didn't budge.

"Damn it!" he shouted.

"Out of the way!" Wilshire said, elbowing him aside.

Rockwell eased backward along the catwalk toward them, firing every step of the way.

The knob made cracking sounds as Wilshire struck it repeatedly with the butt of his rifle.

Rockwell's carbine whirred and the shadows eclipsed the doorway to the outside world.

With a resounding snap, the doorknob broke off, pinged from the catwalk, and careened over the edge. Wilshire raised his right foot and kicked the door once-twice-three times before it swung inward and struck the wall behind it with a thud that made the elevated walkway shiver.

Ramsey ducked past Wilshire as the soldier spun, raised his rifle, and pulled the trigger in one smooth motion. Rockwell was already racing toward them. He dove under Wilshire's muzzle and slid on his chest across the threshold.

The clamor of nails on the iron catwalk filled the air, echoing in the confines.

Wilshire shouted at the top of his lungs and emptied his rifle at the converging shadows as he backed through the doorway.

"Help me move this!" Rockwell shouted, leaning over a heavy wooden desk that had toppled onto its side on the slanted floor.

Ramsey hurried to the opposite end and groaned as he helped Rockwell lift it up onto a bank of file cabinets and maneuver it over what was left of the solitary window. He glanced to his left and saw Wilshire's silhouette trying to wedge the door back into the crooked frame.

The clatter of nails grew deafening as their hunters surged toward the office.

Wilshire shouldered the door and kick-kick-kicked it until it slammed closed.

In the now-complete darkness, Ramsey could hear them on the other side, hurling their bodies against the door.

"Give me a hand!" Wilshire shouted.

Ramsey ran toward the sound of his voice. Wilshire leaned his back against the door, legs braced, trying to maintain his leverage as the door bucked against him. Ramsey shouldered the door, but there was no way they were going to be able to hold them out for long. The repeated impacts on the other side were ferocious and unrelenting, one after another after another. Ramsey already felt his feet slipping. A body struck the door with such force that it opened several inches before slamming closed again.

"Find something to help keep this closed!" Ramsey shouted.

"There's nothing else in here!" Rockwell yelled.

Ramsey heard the *clack-clack-clack* of nails scurrying past him on the other side of the wall. There was a banging sound from the window and the desk toppled inward. A brief influx of gray light around the edges. Ramsey saw a blur of motion as Rockwell launched himself against it, but another blow highlighted the seam around it again. Rockwell didn't have a prayer of holding it up there on his own.

More nails clattered along the walls and across the ceiling above their heads. Scratching, wrenching, gouging their way through the remnants of the roof toward the thin layer of drywall.

They were going to die.

"We have to do this now!" Wilshire shouted.

"And just how the hell are we supposed to get out of here?"

"I know what I'm doing!"

"It's too soon!" Rockwell said. "If we don't get them all, we're dead!"

"We're dead if we wait any longer anyway!"

"What are you talking about?" Ramsey yelled.

The door pounded him from behind and his feet slid. A hand forced its way through the gap. Its claws raked across his face shield. He shoved as hard as he could, but couldn't force the door closed with the wrist in the way. A shrill cry of pain from whatever was attached to the wrist, so loud he could hear it even over the banging and clacking of nails.

"We can't hold them out any longer!" Wilshire shouted. "They'll be through any second now!"

The gap around the desk grew larger as a shadow struggled to slither through. Rockwell bellowed with the effort of trying to hold it in place, a battle he would inevitably lose.

"I'm doing this!" Wilshire yelled.

"Not yet! We don't know where all of them are!"

"In thirty seconds, they'll all be in here!"

"Then we have to wait!"

"We do and we're dead!"

"Whatever you're going to do," Ramsey said, "you'd better do it now!"

"Hold the door!" Wilshire shouted directly into his ear. "You have to buy me time!"

"By myself? There's no way—!"

"Just do it!"

"No!" Rockwell yelled. "It'll be contained in here! It won't get them all!"

"The hell it won't," Wilshire said in an eerily calm voice, and stepped away from the door.

The pressure from the other side knocked Ramsey back into the room. He tried to brace his feet, to gain any kind of leverage, but there was nothing he could do. Bodies forced themselves into the gap, widening it to the point that they were already beginning to shimmy through. Ramsey heard the clatter of nails on the floor directly beside him, claws carving into the trim and the wall, saw flailing appendages pouring through the crack in the dim light.

A glint of metal from the opposite corner of his peripheral vision, where Wilshire crouched over his open backpack. He withdrew the large silver canister he had taken from Moya's belongings. A series of red lights started to blink from a panel on its surface.

"You have to go now," Wilshire said in a voice so soft Ramsey couldn't be sure he had even heard it.

"Are you out of your mind?" Rockwell yelled. "You said you knew what you were doing!"

"I do!"

"You can't trigger it now! We'll all be killed!"

"Then you'd better get going."

"Damn it! We'll find another way!"

"Ten seconds," Wilshire said. "Nine."

Rockwell roared and leapt back from the desk, which tumbled inward after him. His rifle strobed. The sound of gunfire in the small room was like knitting needles piercing Ramsey's eardrums. He screamed in pain and confusion. The rifle spat bullets, not toward the bodies clambering through the window where the desk had been or the gap that Ramsey could no longer seal off, but directly down at the floor at Rockwell's feet.

A solid blow from behind knocked Ramsey forward. He felt the door swing inward behind him, opening the floodgates.

They were going to die.

He stumbled into the middle of the room toward Rockwell, who ceased firing and jumped forward, landing squarely on the floor at the point where gray columns of light erupted through the bullet holes. His entire body passed through with only the slightest resistance. There one moment, gone the next, Rockwell plummeted into the nothingness below.

Ramsey thought of the gaping maw in the ground a story down, of the jagged remains of the roof and the concrete floor standing from it like fangs, of the scorched corpses littering the rubble.

The flashing red beacons illuminated Wilshire as he stood and started firing, his features contorted by rage and terror. The horrible creatures converged on both of them in the flashes of light.

Ramsey cradled his rifle to his chest.

Took a deep breath.

And dropped down through the hole in the floor.

The muzzle of Wilshire's rifle continued to strobe through the rapidly receding, ragged hole above him. He saw Wilshire dive toward the ruined floor. Too late. A flash of brilliant light illuminated the mass of bodies clinging to the sides of the office, scrabbling underneath and over the girders and support framework.

The light pulsed and expanded.

Blinding.

Searing heat.

Rising above him as he fell.

Weightless.

Down.

Down.

Jarring impact.

Stars.

The taste of copper in his mouth.

Black.

VIII

The rhythmic whooshing sound of his pulse in his ears. A tinny hum. Beneath, a voice, calling to him from across a great distance, the words incomprehensible.

His eyelids part. Crescents of searing light. He closes them again.

Whoooosh. Whoooosh. Whoooosh.

The pain. It ripples up his spine and drives a spike into the base of his skull. He whimpers and his mouth fills with blood. A cough, uncontrollable. Warmth on his face, running down his cheeks.

The voice again. Closer. Distorted by the tinnitus in his inner ear.

Whoooosh. Whoooosh. Whoooosh.

He opens his eyes again. Spears of gray light, lancing straight through his pounding head. A shadow, its outline hazy, incorporeal.

Sensation in his extremities, dull, throbbing. He's reminded of his legs, his arms. Pins and needles in his digits. Heat. The trickle of sweat.

Whoooosh. Whoooosh. Whoooosh.

The voice. Deep, resonant, ricocheting inside his head with the Doppler Effect.

He remembers. He remembers the light. Falling. The shadows.

Dear God. The shadows.

His rifle. Where is his rifle? It was in his hands. Where are his hands?

He sputters. More warmth on his face.

The voice.

"Take it easy. Don't try to get up too quickly."

Pressure under his shoulders, easing him up from the ground.

He's sitting, the blood racing away from his head. Dizzy.

His eyes roll upward...

"Stay with me, Dr. Ramsey."

The light, no longer blinding. Weak. It's dark, not dark. Dim. The man in front of him. Shadow, not shadow. Rockwell. His silhouette. Blurry, not blurry. Smoke. A cloud of smoke hanging over him. Moving between them, through them.

"What...?" The word forms, drips from his mouth on more warmth.

The arm under his back, guiding him, lifting him to his feet. There they are. He sways, but Rockwell helps him ride it out. Dizziness fades. Not the pain. The pain is sharp. It helps to focus his mind.

Make it stop!

His vision clears.

Small fires burn around him, flames flickering on the floor. Above him. He looks up and sees the office burning, now little more than a skeleton of scorched iron and smoldering timber.

"Wilshire?" he whispers.

Rockwell shakes his head. The shield over his face is cracked, spider-webbing his features, which shimmer with a crimson skein.

"How...?" He shakes his head to clear it, to free the words. "The explosion...what...?"

"Semtex," Rockwell says as he turns away and walks into the swirling smoke. His disembodied voice trails him. "We need to hurry. We're totally out of time."

Ramsey glances at his personal dosimeter.

50 milliSeiverts per hour.

One-seventh of the rate at Chernobyl.

Acute radiation sickness would soon set in.

Nausea. Vomiting. Hemorrhaging. Erythema.

Hurry was an understatement.

~*~

Ramsey's head was pounding and he felt sick to his stomach. He couldn't be certain whether it was a consequence of the fall, the radiation, or of what he was seeing right now. He walked through the aftermath as if through a dream. There were flames all around him, barely visible, lurking beneath the roiling black smoke of their own creation. Chunks of flaming debris still rained from the cantilevered office above him, striking the floor with explosions of glowing cinders. If there were any remains up there, he couldn't see them. Whatever had once been Wilshire was now undoubtedly vaporized. Ramsey had tried to ascend the iron staircase, but the soles of his boots had begun to melt immediately and he feared compromising the integrity of his suit. That close to the heart of the blast, Wilshire would surely have been incinerated, but they owed it to him to continue to look for as long as possible. After all, it was the least they could do considering he had sacrificed his life for them. But they wouldn't be able to search for much longer. They were already risking the stochastic effects of the radiation as it was. And the detonation would not have gone unnoticed. Soon, the entire area would be crawling with North Korean soldiers and—

Another boom of rifle fire.

The report echoed in what remained of the warehouse before rolling out through the demolished wall and across the surrounding field like thunder.

That made three survivors now. Three of more than he cared to count.

He shuffled through the smoke toward the origin of the sound and found Rockwell still standing over the body. His suit was spattered with blood that had already begun to clot with ash and dust. Ramsey placed his palm on Rockwell's shoulder. Rockwell nodded before shrugging out from beneath it and walking away.

Ramsey stared down at the corpse sprawled before him.

Flames flickered from the ragged remnants of the clothing that reminded him of hospital issue-surgical scrubs. The skin beneath was scorched black, cracked, oozing amber pustulates. The small, bare feet were scabbed and riddled with briars and thorns. Caked with mud and soot. Elongated toes with hooked talons that doubled their overall length. Big toes that projected sideways from the others, opposable. The hands were slightly more proportionate, the claws merely sharp extensions of the existing nails. The fur on the arms and chest, the long hair on the head, all singed back to the skin. But it was the face that got to him. To both of them.

It was the face of a child.

Wide eyes shot through with vessels, golden irises rimmed with scarlet, too large. Even in death they reflected the light, like those of a nocturnal predator, which was obviously what this poor creature had been engineered to be. Tiny, bulbous nose. Lips barely able to accommodate the protruding chimp-like teeth. Only longer and sharper, more like those of a jungle cat. Whether more primate than human was irrelevant. They were still juveniles. Still children, for Christ's sake. Bred to kill in a lab now collapsed beneath their feet. In defiance of the laws of man, of the Geneva Convention, of the will of God.

What had been the goal? To raise an army? To augment an existing one? To use this arcane knowledge to convert soldiers into an unstoppable force?

Ramsey prayed he would never know, for at what cost had this knowledge been obtained? What did this say about mankind as a whole that it was willing to subject its own progeny, if that was indeed what these creatures were, to such reprehensible experimentation?

He looked away before he could dwell on the hole in its forehead, the tattoo of gunpowder around it, the blossoms of bone and gray matter that had been the only small measure of compassion bestowed upon this pitiful creation in its entire miserable life.

A whimpering sound through the smoke. To his left. No. Behind him and to his right. God, how many more survived the explosion? Couldn't they have been granted one solitary mercy?

He stepped over severed appendages. Slender arms, the meat smoldering. Stubby legs that seemed to fold upon themselves. What he could only assume were the vestiges of tails. Flames slowly consumed the flesh, exposing the charred framework of bones.

Rockwell's silhouette towered over a supine form. It raised the stump of an arm in a feeble attempt to ward off the rifle directed at its head. The whimper became a shrill screech that was joined by several more from somewhere in the smoke.

Ramsey wished he could remove his helmet, if only to clap his hands over his ears.

A flash of muzzle flare. A resounding boom.

The screeching ceased, and again there was only whimpering.

And beneath it, a new sound materialized. From far away. He felt it as much as heard it. A faint rumble that made the ground tremble ever so slightly.

He glanced at Rockwell, who stood stock-still for a moment, like a prairie dog at the mouth of its burrow, then sprinted toward the demolished wall.

The rumble grew louder. As it did, it dissociated into the metered rhythm of a racing heartbeat, a steady, unmistakable *whupp-whupp-whupp*. More than one. There were several helicopters streaking directly toward them from the south, still invisible through the smoke, beyond the tree line.

"We have to go," Ramsey whispered.

"Not yet," Rockwell said. "This has to end here and now."

"If we're still here when they arrive..."

Ramsey couldn't bring himself to finish the sentence.

"Then so be it," Rockwell said. He looked directly at Ramsey, defiantly. There were tears on the hardened soldier's face. "You go. I can finish this on my own."

"No," Ramsey whispered. "Like you said, this has to end here."

They fanned out around the ruined warehouse, following the cries of the survivors even as the thumping sound of blades drowned them out.

Ramsey sobbed as he euthanized one, the combination of sheer terror and primal rage in its bright eyes forever to be a soul-deep wound that would never heal.

The smoke swirled around him now. The rotor wash whipped him harder and harder until he could barely stand. A searchlight passed over him, stretching his shadow across the carnage. At any second, bullets would tear up the ground around him and chew right through him. It was over. All over. Only one thing left to do. He whirled toward the chopper, raised his rifle, and bellowed as he squeezed—

"No!" Rockwell shouted, forcing the barrel of his rifle down. "Hold your fire!"

Ramsey raised his hand to shield his eyes from the blinding light. He could only stare as the sleek MH-60 Direct Action Penetrator, a modified Blackhawk, hovered momentarily before setting down on the ground above him where the building had once been level with the earth. The second chopper beat a circuit around the warehouse several times before touching down on the opposite side of the building, barely visible through the broken windows.

"They're ours," Rockwell said. The relief in his voice was palpable. "They're American."

Ramsey fell to his knees amid the wreckage and watched in wonder as an armed soldier wearing a similar hazard suit to his own sprinted down the hillside toward them.

"The North Koreans are about ten minutes out," the man shouted over the ceaseless thunder of the chopper. "We have to move! Now!"

The man grabbed Ramsey by the arm and tugged him to his feet. Ramsey felt numb as he stumbled out of the ruined building and up the steep slope.

He had been certain he was going to die.

Now he moved as if through a dream. The world stopped turning beneath him. The rotors slowed, their thumping pulse in time with his own. The men were shouting, but he couldn't understand their words. A chaos of white noise. Churning smoke. His sole focus was on the helicopter. He ran. Tripped. Fell. Ran again into the white glare of the searchlight. Another man, a shadow, appeared and pulled him toward freedom.

"We have to hurry, Dr. Ramsey," he said, and ushered Ramsey toward the open side door.

Ramsey glanced back down the hill toward the collapsed building. Men moved through the smoke, ghosts formed of darkness, alternately hidden and then revealed.

And in that moment before he was shoved up and into the chopper, he could have sworn he heard a primate scream.

IX

The following hours passed in a blur. Ramsey vaguely remembered flying so low over the dense forests that he worried they would tear off their landing gear in the branches. Wending through steep valleys. Mirroring the topography closely until they crossed the border into South Korea and then finally rising back onto radar and streaking toward the base from which he had originally been dispatched in Kansŏng. He'd been whisked from the chopper to a transport carrier that lifted off even before he was out of his protective suit. A medic had been waiting with an IV to hydrate him and a kit of needles to draw samples of his blood, but all Ramsey had wanted to do was sleep. The whole ordeal had seemed like a nightmare, a memory of events that could have happened to someone else entirely, when he was awakened upon landing at a tiny, unnamed Air Force Base on an anonymous island that looked like every other along the Pacific rim and transferred to the two-story base hospital for a more thorough evaluation.

He now rested in a firm bed with sunlight streaming through the gap in the blinds onto the blankets over his legs. Its warmth was a sensation beyond belief. Outside the window, tropical trees with purple and red blossoms swayed against the placid backdrop of the turquoise ocean.

After so many time zone changes and sleepless nights, he had no idea what time it was, or even what day.

All he knew was that his ordeal was now over and his normal life would soon resume.

He found the remote control and clicked on the television mounted to the otherwise bare white wall. Took a drink of the ice water on the stand beside his bed. Wondered what was on the menu for breakfast. Or was it lunch? Surely there was a clock around here somewhere.

"...*have suddenly and visibly begun to stand down,*" the polished voice of a newscaster said. Ramsey glanced up to see the CNN logo at the bottom corner of the screen. A parade of stock quotes scrolled past under footage of convoys of Jeeps rolling down highways interspersed with uniformed soldiers clambering into covered ground transport vehicles. "*This coming on the heels of the statement issued by Kim Jong-un, Supreme Leader of the Democratic People's Republic of Korea, in which he categorically redacted his initial allegations that the Republic of Korea was responsible for the unprovoked nuclear detonation on its soil. While details are still forthcoming, Kim has scheduled a brief press conference in a matter of hours in regard to what he has termed an 'unfortunate and unforeseeable accident' at a formerly classified nuclear storage facility near Kŭmgang-ŭp. Critics decry Kim's odd and seemingly inexplicable eleventh-hour statement as disingenuous and call for him to be held accountable for the deaths of more than a hundred refugees reportedly overcome by the fallout, but United Nations officials have quickly, and somewhat surprisingly, risen to his defense in a prepared address delivered by Security Council President Anders Odegaard.*"

The footage cut to a tall man with silver hair and piercing blue eyes behind a podium featuring the U.N. crest.

"*At this point, we have no reason to believe that Mr. Kim had been anything other than forthcoming. Considering that all involved at the site were killed in the tragedy, we find Mr. Kim's claims that he was forced to act without the benefit of all of the facts to be plausible, if not entirely regrettable. And while we commend him on staying the launch of a full scale assault against the Republic of Korea while awaiting the results of further investigation, we find his knee-jerk response to the situation troubling, to say the least. To his credit, Mr. Kim has agreed to grant U.N. inspectors full access to any and all facilities involved in the production, enrichment, and potential weaponization of nuclear-grade material.*"

Cut to images of more armed soldiers, some of them with patches featuring the red and gold of the Chinese flag and others with the red and blue yin-yang of the Republic of Korea.

"Despite the support of the U.N. Security Council, Chinese and South Korean forces remain mobilized, albeit in slowly diminishing numbers. A formal press release from Beijing, written in an arguably disappointed tone, offered a timetable for the withdrawal of Chinese troops from staging grounds across its southern border, but President Hu Jintao, as of yet, has declined to lower his country's overall state of preparedness pending an agreement with the U.N. to allow his own experts to participate in their investigation. South Korean President Lee, understandably, isn't quite as willing to adopt the same forgive-and-forget mentality as the rest of the world, saying that 'they weren't the ones who had a nuclear bomb detonated in their backyard.'"

Another cut. A sunken warehouse, smoke billowing from its collapsed roof. A shaky recording from high above. The shadow of a helicopter passing over the slanted ground of a crater.

Ramsey's heart nearly stopped in his chest.

"This is the first footage captured of the Kangwŏn-do site, provided by North Korean officials, showing a facility which, at least superficially, appears to have no direct military applications. And while radiation levels are already plummeting, due in large measure to the subterranean nature of the detonation, conservative estimates suggest that it will still be more than twenty-four hours before levels are considered safe for the U.N. envoy—"

A knock at the door. Ramsey glanced to his left in time to see the door swing inward.

Rockwell stepped into the room. When Ramsey had found himself on the plane without Rockwell, he had assumed he'd never see the soldier again. He was wearing a pair of clean fatigues that somehow made him look much smaller than he had in the field. Ramsey almost didn't recognize him without the black greasepaint on his face.

Rockwell offered a twitch of the left corner of his mouth.

"That burn will leave a nice tan when it fades," Ramsey said.

"Erythema. Thanks to the radiation and a cracked face shield. I have a good mind to sue."

He gestured to the lone chair beside the bed. Ramsey nodded and Rockwell plopped down with a sigh, then inclined his head toward the TV.

"I see you've found the political spin channel."

"It's making me dizzy just watching it. Next thing you know that warehouse will have been a facility for breeding puppies and cloning rainbows."

"I can only imagine the expression on Kim's face when he took the call from the U.N.. Face an international tribunal to answer for violations of the Geneva Convention or back down with a small measure of his dignity intact."

"They had him by the short-hairs, all right."

Rockwell nodded and kept his eyes on the television. There was obviously something on his mind, but he wasn't quite sure how to begin. Ramsey waited him out.

"Have you been debriefed yet?"

"Not officially, but I'd imagine someone will be coming by shortly to threaten to cut out my tongue." Ramsey smirked. "We were never there, I assume."

"Never where?"

Rockwell looked at his hands in his lap as though to make sure they weren't shaking.

"You suck at small talk," Ramsey said. "Just cut to the chase."

Rockwell glanced up into each corner of the room in turn, then at the heating ducts, the lamp on the nightstand, and the TV like he was looking for something specific.

"There are some things…" he said in little more than a whisper. He paused as though debating how to continue. "Some things that bother me. That just don't sit right with me, you know?"

Ramsey wasn't quite certain what to say, so he simply gestured for Rockwell to proceed.

"Remember those footprints we followed from the refugee camp toward the detonation site?" He waited for a nod of acknowledgement. "They were indistinct, right? Traveling single file, one on top of another. We couldn't really tell how many of them there were. We just assumed they belonged to whatever was responsible for the slaughter. It made sense at the time. It was the only logical option, right?"

"I don't see—" Rockwell shushed him and glanced again around the room. Ramsey continued in a whisper. "I don't see where you're going with this."

"We wondered why they weren't traveling through the trees since they could obviously do so with such ease. You even posed that question at the time. And we saw all of those branches carved up by their claws. Why would they try to hide their numbers on the ground when they made no effort at all to do so in the trees?"

Ramsey sat up and leaned forward in the bed.

"Did you get a good look at their feet?" Rockwell asked.

Ramsey thought about the bare feet with the opposable big toes and the long claws.

"I grew up in Tennessee," Rockwell said. "I spent weeks at a time in the Great Smoky Mountains with my old man during hunting season. Deer, boars, black bears. We shot them all. Mainly with bows. We had to track them, you know? And bears? They're not going to wander up on you in the middle of the woods. You have to recognize the signs. Scat. Scratch marks on the tree trunks. Paw prints, even on bare, dry ground. The pads of their toes. They leave distinct marks. Teardrop-shaped because of the claws. Those tracks we were following back in Korea? They didn't have that shape. We just didn't know we should have been looking for it at the time. The signs were all around us in the trees. We just flat out missed them."

"Where are you going with this?" Ramsey whispered, but he already had a hunch. He could feel it coming together, a tingle at the base of his skull. He swung his legs over the side of the bed so that he was right next to Rockwell. "You aren't suggesting—?"

"Think about it. Looking back, it's clear as day. The clues were there all along. Remember what happened to Moya? Remember the sound of the gunfire? Tap. Tap-tap-tap. Tap. Then nothing. Two weapons. One set for single fire, the other triple. There was just so much blood we must have missed it. And his wounds. They weren't the same as those of the refugees, were they? In every instance, the killers went for the side of the neck, nearly tore the whole damn thing off. But Moya? Not even a nibble. And how long did it take those creatures to come after us? We thought we were outsmarting them by sneaking around through the forest. Think about how much time we had with Moya's body. It wasn't because we fooled them. It was because they weren't anywhere near us at the time."

"So you're saying—?"

"Those helicopters arrived at precisely the perfect moment, didn't they? The North Koreans were only ten minutes out, or at least that's what we were told. How did the pilots know where to find us? We were totally off the grid. From the time of the explosion that cost Wilshire his life to their arrival couldn't have been more than half an hour. And how long did it take us to get from there to Kansŏng?"

"Longer than that."

"Which means that they were already in the air when Wilshire triggered the detonation. And think about the overall appearance of the situation. Blackhawks streaking across the border would have been perceived as an all-out act of aggression. We discussed that, remember? Those choppers wouldn't have been dispatched without some sort of guarantee that if they were detected it wouldn't be the start of World War Three. What was that guarantee? What was the one thing we could hold over Kim's head that would force him to back down? The nuclear detonation that triggered this whole mess? What was the reason behind it? We knew we could back them down because we would have the proof we needed, the smoking gun we could tie directly to Kim to have him tried for crimes against humanity, but we could also use that leverage in a positive manner, couldn't we? We could make that little problem he was trying to cover up go away for him and allow him to save face. And what was that guarantee? What undeniable physical proof did we need to have?"

"The bodies," Ramsey said. "We needed the mutated bodies."

"And how did the Americans know? How did they know where to dispatch the choppers? How did they know when we physically encountered the creatures?"

"Jesus. There were already men on the ground," Ramsey said. His heart was pounding now, his brain firing at a million miles an hour. "It was their tracks we were following. But why wouldn't they just do the whole thing themselves? I mean, if they were already there and no one else knew about it, why did they need us at all?"

"Because we were there under the U.N. flag. We were nothing more than a smokescreen. Think about it. The U.N. can then approach the North Koreans with the proof on behalf of one hundred and ninety-five countries and take a globally unified approach. America, acting alone, would be perceived as an aggressor, its actions a declaration of war. By letting the U.N. step to the forefront, America's able to maintain the moral high ground. So why were they really there when we were essentially led right to our goal, when the U.N. would be given all of the credit for the success of the mission, when they could have easily claimed it for themselves?" His voice had risen steadily. He caught himself, drew a deep breath, and moderated his tone again. "Why were they really there?"

"They didn't want anyone, not even the U.N., to know they had an operation of their own underway."

"Why?"

"Because for whatever reason they feared it wouldn't be sanctioned."

"And what possible reason could there be for that?"

The answer hit Ramsey like an uppercut to the chin.

"You said you knew about the nature of the experimentation going on in that facility. It stands to reason that if you knew, they did too. They were there because of those experiments. They were there for the biotechnology."

"And while we were airlifted out of there on the first chopper—"

"They were loading up the other one on the back side of the building."

Rockwell sighed and rubbed his bloodshot eyes. After a long moment of silence, he finally stood and looked down at Ramsey with a newfound expression of determination.

Ramsey summoned one of his own to match it.

"You didn't come down here just to walk me through your conclusion, did you?" Ramsey whispered. "You want to do something about it. And you need my help. What's the plan?"

"We make them pay for what they did."

"And just how do you propose we do that?"

"The equipment you had in the field. If I can get it from your pack, can you make it work without drawing any unnecessary attention to what we're doing?"

"Yeah, but…what do you have in mind?"

"Remember that object I took from Moya after he died?"

EPILOGUE

United States Army Bioengineering
Research & Development Laboratory

Ft. Detrick, Maryland

May 25

7:55 p.m. EST

Ramsey had been so focused on achieving success that he never paused to contemplate what came *after*. It was always a matter of researching and testing and making his project work. He knew he would eventually pull it off, but until he returned to Ft. Detrick, he'd never considered how that triumph would affect his life. He hadn't expected to be paraded around the base on the shoulders of his envious colleagues any more than he had planned to find the Nobel Prize waiting on his desk for him. He simply hadn't thought that far ahead at all. If he had, he might not have been in such a rush to get back to his lab. Maybe he would have spent at least a few days touring the islands, perhaps swing up the west coast and check out the Pacific Northwest when he hit the mainland. What had been waiting for him, while entirely logical and should have been expected, was the last thing in the world he was prepared to handle.

Work.

More work than he had ever thought possible.

Once word had gone out that his project was fully functional, the lab had turned into a madhouse. Bodies arrived on planes day and night. And not just bodies. Parts. Heads mostly, but occasionally just eyes. The cooler was so jam-packed with them that the major general himself had been forced to intercede and establish a system of prioritization. And Ramsey had begun to suspect that Staff Sergeant Corvo, who was charged with cadaver duty, was actively plotting against him. He was more miserable than ever, thanks to the repulsive stench that seemed to cling to him wherever he went. Once Corvo heard that the other men were calling him Sergeant Cornhole, if he hadn't already, Ramsey figured he'd better start sleeping with one eye open. But he knew that the USAMRMC wasn't about to let anything happen to him. They had big plans for their golden boy. Yes, indeed. They were going to work him like no man had ever been worked before. They were going to work him until he died on his feet, and then they were going to work him some more. At this point, Ramsey was rooting for that to happen sooner than later.

He rubbed his weary eyes and killed the last of the cold, stale coffee. Was that the third or the fourth pot of the day? What day was it anyway? Maybe he had a few minutes to slip outside to see the sun, if it was still up, get some fresh air—

The door exploded inward with the sound of a shotgun blast. Ramsey flinched like he always did and Corvo smirked like he always did, as was their routine. Ramsey's new lab was much bigger than his old one, a real step up in the world. Aldridge had gone out of his way to equip this one with the nicest computers and printers, the fanciest components, and room to add several new Hindsight stations. And, of course, swinging doors like they used in emergency rooms, because taking the time to turn a single goddamn doorknob would simply slow down Ramsey's pace too much.

"Break time's over, Dr. Frankenstein," Corvo said, shoving the gurney into the room. He made sure to collide with every object he possibly could on his way to Ramsey's station. "Got some new meat for you. Fresh, never frozen."

"Thank you, Sergeant Corn—" Ramsey hoped he caught himself in time. "—vo. Corvo."

The expression on the staff sergeant's face as he ducked back out of the lab let him know that he hadn't.

Ramsey unzipped the body bag on the cart and recoiled from the scent. Corvo was right. This one couldn't have been dead for more than a day, at the most. He smelled smoke and burnt hair. Ramsey was already reaching for the eye tongs when he caught a glimpse of the man's face and froze. He stared at it long and hard, scrutinizing the ridge of the brow, the cut of the jaw, the color of the skin beneath the smudges of ash, the entry wound through his right temple and the massive exit wound above and behind his left ear. There was something familiar about the man, but not something he could readily place...

God, he was too tired to be doing this. How many had he done so far today? Thirty? Thirty-five? He had to be well over three hundred now in not even two full weeks since his return from South Korea—

That was it. He recognized this man, all right. No doubt about it. The gunshot wound made sense, but why did the corpse smell like smoke?

Ramsey hit the button on the intercom and removed the cadaver's right eye while he waited for a response. The lateral orbital rim was fractured, which made the extraction difficult, but he always used the right eye for consistency's sake, a routine that had started with a young girl on a blood-drenched field a world away.

"What do you want now?" Corvo replied from the speaker mount.

"Did this one arrive with any paperwork?"

"They all arrive with paperwork. Since when do you care?"

"Would you mind bringing it to me?"

"Seriously? I just sat down for like the first time all fuc—"

Ramsey terminated the conversation with his elbow.

He'd performed this procedure so many times now that he could do it in his sleep. He had the entire system set up and functioning in a matter of minutes. The image was already running the gamut of filters when Corvo burst through the doors with a printout in his hand. He tossed it onto the dead man's chest and blew back out through the doors without a word, which was totally unlike Corvo.

Ramsey definitely needed to watch his back now.

The computer beeped to signal the completion of the process. Ramsey sent the finished image to the printer with the tap of a key. He was too busy reading through the printout to look at the computer monitor.

There was no information whatsoever. No name. No date of birth. Nothing. All the form contained was the various tracking numbers and the signatures of those along the chain of custody for the remains. And still this corpse had been bumped to the front of the line. Whoever this man was, someone out there wanted answers about his death in a hurry and had the political capital to make it happen. The body was still so fresh that were it not for the gunshot wound that had taken off the better part of his cranium, the man looked as though he could have crawled right off the table and walked away, unlike the majority of the "blue men" who Corvo ferried back and forth from the cooler.

Ramsey cast the useless printout onto the work station beside him, where someone had apparently dropped off a letter for him while he was otherwise occupied or, more likely, on one of his countless trips down the hall to the restroom, thanks to the diuretic effects of the coffee. Who dropped it off? When had they done so? It was almost as though someone had deliberately placed it where only he would see it, but when no one else was around to bear witness.

There was no return address on the small envelope. No postage. Just one handwritten word.

Ramsey.

He picked it up and turned it over and over in his hands, his brow furrowed, then looked from the letter to the corpse and back again. He opened it with a wry smile on his face.

Inside was a small newspaper clipping, little more than a passing mention, roughly the size of the Post-it note stuck to it. The note read simply:

It's over now.

The whirring sound of the photo printer ceased. Ramsey skimmed the article as he crossed the room to where the image from the dead man's eye waited. There had been a fire at a warehouse near Dulles International Airport outside of Washington, D.C.

shortly before midnight. While there was no immediate confirmation of human casualties, authorities reported that the remains of several rare and unusual primates had been found amid the blackened debris. An investigation would be launched posthaste into what officials believed to be a smuggling operation involving endangered species, which fetched huge dollars on the black market.

Ramsey set the article aside, removed the photograph from the printer, and walked back to his personal desk in the rear corner of the lab. He plopped down in his chair, set the image on his keyboard, and opened the top drawer. There was a nondescript manila envelope shuffled into the mess of papers and folders inside. He withdrew it, set it on his lap, and stared at it for a long moment before he finally opened it and extricated the lone piece of paper inside. He positioned it on his desk directly to the left of the image he had just produced. The paper was crumpled, the quality of the image pathetic by comparison to the new one beside it, but it was still clear enough to show Ramsey what he needed to see.

The blindspot was a black hole in the bottom left portion of the picture. The remainder was pixelated and hazy due to decomposition. The image was dark, yet he could still discern the forest, the broad leaves of the maples and the brushy branches of the pines. And the tiny gray ring hidden in their midst, from which a curl of gray smoke rose. It was the barrel of a rifle, nearly invisible, like the man who braced it against his shoulder, only the whites of his eyes clearly evident. But the shape of his features...the sharp crest of his brow, the outline of his bulging jaw...highlighted ever so subtly by the flash of the muzzle flare...were identical to those of the corpse across the room from him now.

This was the last thing that United Nations Peacekeeper Eduard Moya had seen before he died.

Ramsey shifted his gaze to the right and looked at the new image for the first time. The ink was still damp and glistened under the bright lights. Flames filled the right half of the image, rising from crates and boxes, and from a furry lump on what looked like a stainless steel table. The killer had stood in precisely such a way that the black circle of the blindspot hid his face, chest, and the majority of his right arm, all except for the nine-millimeter pistol directed straight at Ramsey through the picture. And the left arm, which offered a discreet thumbs-up gesture where only the dead man, or someone looking through his right eye, would see it.

"Right back at you, Rockwell," Ramsey said through a crooked grin.

ABOUT THE AUTHOR

Michael McBride is the author of *Bloodletting, Burial Ground, Innocents Lost, Predatory Instinct,* and half of *The Mad & The Macabre* (with Jeff Strand). He lives in Westminster, Colorado with his wife and children. To learn more about the author and his other works visit www.michaelmcbride.net.

Made in the USA
Columbia, SC
27 January 2021